GONE

ONE MOMENT THEY WERE THERE...

ANNA-MARIE MORGAN

Copyright © 2018 by Anna-marie Morgan

All rights reserved.

No part of this book may be reproduced in any form or by any electronic or mechanical means, including information storage and retrieval systems, without written permission from the author, except for the use of brief quotations in a book review.

❦ Created with Vellum

*This one is for my readers,
especially those who have read every book in the series.
Thank you for your support.*

ALSO IN THIS SERIES:

Death Master
You Will Die
Total Wipeout
Deep Cut
The Pusher

Coming Soon:
The Crossbow Killer

1

THE GIRL AT THE BUS STOP

It is amazing how much of a person's condition can be gleaned by that initial glance. A coat too thin to resist January's bite. Shoes worn. Blonde hair unkempt. A young girl lost. But pretty. The girl was pretty. A runaway reading a magazine at a bus stop. Her breath an ephemeral cloud around her head.

Eighty-one-year-old Sheila Jones was about to go back to her weeding of dead leaves and woody stems, when the girl looked up. A smile warmed her young features and she raised her hand in a wave. Sheila waved back. Fourteen. The girl looked about fourteen.

For a moment, Sheila considered taking her a bigger coat. Something worth wearing. But the girl had already returned to her magazine and Sheila thought better of it. The bus to Newtown would be along in just a couple of minutes. The older woman went back to her clearing work.

The bus shuddered around the corner and Sheila straightened up, pleased the girl would finally be able to get into somewhere warm. But, she wasn't there. Sheila blinked. Definitely not there. The bus rolled on without stopping, clouds of diesel smoke fluttering the pages of the discarded magazine.

Sheila reached for her walking cane and headed towards the gate at the bottom of her garden, directly overlooking the road. She checked left and right, as far as she could see, but there was no-one. She walked the few yards to the bus stop and picked up the dog-eared magazine, discarded mid-story. She saw what looked like a fresh droplet of blood.

If it were not for that blood, she would have most likely forgotten about it. Or else, wondered if she had imagined the girl. She could count on her fingers the number of times she had seen a stranger at that bus stop and they had never before disappeared.

"MORNING, MA'AM." Dewi gave a broad smile and placed a coffee to one side of his DI.

"Good morning, Dewi." Yvonne smiled back, feeling as relaxed as she had for a while. "Where's the DCI? I thought he was going to brief us?"

"He had to go out. Didn't tell me where. He did, however, give me an address he'd like us to check out. Someone reported an abduction, apparently. Wants us to take a look."

"An abduction? What abduction?"

"I've no idea. It was the first I'd heard of it." Dewi sipped his coffee and winced at the heat. "I watched the local news, too. No abduction mentioned on there."

Yvonne shrugged. "No worries. Where are we going?"

"Dolfor."

"Right. Drink up. We'd best be on it."

WITHIN HALF-AN-HOUR, THEY WERE OUTSIDE SHEILA JONES'

cottage, taking in the well-kept hedges and neat borders. A path that was free of weeds. A topiary plant either side of the doorstep. Everything in its place.

Sheila appeared at the door, as neat and orderly as her garden. Although clearly advanced in years, the frail lady wore her hair in a carefully arranged bun. Dressed in pale blue, she smelled of a mixture of soap and fabric conditioner. Her wizened eyes shone and it was clear from her stare that Sheila Jones was in full possession of her probably considerable faculties.

"Pleased to meet you." She held out a tremulous hand.

Yvonne took it, simultaneously pulling out her warrant card. "Likewise. We're from-"

Sheila had turned away, towards her sitting room. "I know who you are." She raised a hand and waved it, still looking ahead of her. "I've been expecting you."

The DI shot a sideways glance at Dewi, who shrugged.

Sheila's living room had a surprisingly modern feel. Sisal carpet and a cream and beige colour scheme. She motioned them to sit. "My daughter helped decorate." She smiled at Yvonne, as though reading her thoughts.

Yvonne smiled back. "Your daughter has good taste."

Dewi took out his notepad. "You telephoned about an abduction you witnessed."

"Yes." Sheila placed a supportive hand to her lower back, as settled herself into an armchair next to the window.

"Can you tell us who was abducted?"

Sheila frowned. "I... I don't know who she was. Only that she was a stranger to the village and that she was down on her luck."

Dewi looked up from his note-taking, a frown darkening his face.

Yvonne took over. "Tell us what happened, Mrs Jones."

Sheila sighed. "I was in my garden. Just doing some tidying up and I saw a young girl, around fourteen years old, standing at the bus stop. She was reading a magazine."

"You said she wasn't from around here..." Yvonne encouraged.

"She looked as though she'd been living rough."

"What makes you say that?" Dewi resumed writing.

"Her hair was ruffled, maybe knotted. She wasn't properly dressed for the weather." Sheila sighed again and rubbed her chin. "Now that I'm saying it out loud, I feel foolish."

"What colour was her hair?" Yvonne tilted her head to one side.

"A mousey sort of blonde. She was reading a magazine," Sheila repeated.

"What happened then? Tell us about the abduction. What did you see?"

Sheila paused, biting her lip. "I didn't exactly *see* anything. It's more what I didn't see."

Dewi cleared his throat.

Yvonne leaned towards the elderly woman, her gaze intense. "What do you mean?"

"One moment she was waiting for the bus to come along and waving at me, and the next...she was gone. When the bus did come along, it didn't stop. It just carried on towards Newtown."

Dewi sighed. "Does it get lonely out here, Mrs Jones?"

Sheila winced and Yvonne shot her sergeant a stern look.

Mrs Jones continued. "I went out to the gate. Looked both ways along the road and there was no girl. Then, I saw her magazine at the roadside. I picked it up. That's when I saw the blood."

"What blood?" Dewi raised both eyebrows.

Sheila pointed to her oak coffee table. "It's on there."

Yvonne rose from her seat to retrieve the magazine. The pages were scrunched and there was a partial muddy footprint on one corner of the opened page. In the middle crease, lay a single drop of dried blood, about a half-centimetre in diameter.

"The droplet was still wet, when I picked up the magazine." Sheila's eye contact was steady.

"Did you notice if any cars went past the bus stop, Mrs Jones?" Yvonne turned the magazine over, noting that it was 'Take a Break', and had been left in the middle of a story of forbidden love. "Could it be that someone just stopped to pick her up? A friend, perhaps?"

"I think a few cars went by. I didn't see any of them. I wasn't watching her, after she waved at me, until I heard the bus approaching and noticed she had gone. So, I'm afraid I can't give you descriptions of the vehicles."

"May we take the magazine?" Yvonne withdrew an evidence packet from her bag.

"Yes, of course. Are you going to look into it?" Sheila's eyes flicked back and fore across the DI's face.

"Yes," Yvonne said simply, avoiding looking in Dewi's direction. She sensed he was less than impressed.

"Then I am happy." Sheila smiled, though there was still a stiffness in the muscles around her eyes.

2

A TENTATIVE BEGINNING

"Seriously?" Dewi stood next to the car, hands on hips.

"What?" Yvonne pressed her key fob and opened the driver's door.

"Misleading her like that."

"I wasn't misleading her, Dewi."

"She didn't see an abduction. There's nothing for us to *look into*." Dewi climbed into his seat and clicked his seatbelt on.

"Technically, no. We don't have much to go on."

"We don't have anything to go on. The girl was probably thumbing a lift, or else a friend passed by and picked her up. That'll be why no-one's reported her missing. I suspect Mrs Jones spends too much time on her own."

Yvonne nodded, as she fired up the engine. "There's probably nothing to see here, I agree. And yet, Sheila Jones strikes me as an intelligent woman and something spooked her. Besides, we have a discarded magazine with blood on it."

Dewi laughed. "Come on, Yvonne. Magazines get discarded all the time."

"Yes, but usually *after* someone's finished the story. I don't know any girls who get into reading a love story and don't read through to the end."

"Are you yanking my chain?" Dewi pulled a face.

The DI grinned. "A little. You get so serious. But, I think we should keep our ears to the ground. We'll write up our notes and keep them safe and ask if a couple of uniform guys can go around the village asking whether anyone else saw anything suspicious. Then, if someone *is* reported missing, we'll have a head start. Oh, and get the blood tested for gender and a DNA profile if they can get one." She flicked her DS a quick look and shrugged. "Just in case."

THAT AFTERNOON, the DI was back. Alone, this time. She left her car in a lay-by a few hundred yards from Sheila's home and wandered the road that meandered through the tiny hamlet. She walked for around a thousand yards in both directions, seeing only road, hedges and animals grazing stumps in the muddy fields. What she didn't see, was another person. Not anywhere. Lights were on in a couple of the houses. The sky was darkening. No-one was about. No wonder the appearance and disappearance of the young girl had stood out so poignantly to Sheila Jones.

A mist was gathering. It's cold, wispy tendrils reached out towards her. She fastened her cream, woollen coat, lifting its collar to better shelter her neck. A deep shiver travelled the length of her spine. Glancing up at the darkening sky, she turned back in the direction of her vehicle.

3

DREAD

Donna held her breath. She could hear the men arguing. At least, she thought they were arguing. The voices were louder this time, though they were still muffled by thick walls. She wondered if they were the same men who had taken her. The voices were getting louder, accompanied by the occasional loud bang. Something being slammed on a table. Donna cowered, still sore from being backhanded across the jaw. She could taste the tangy blood from her swollen lips and feel a throbbing in the back of her head. She hadn't seen the face of her attacker. He had worn a white, angular mask inside of a charcoal-black, hooded top.

She thought she heard someone cry out. Were there others here? Others like her? She'd seen barely a soul for days. On the couple of occasions they had checked on her, the masked men refused to answer her desperate question - why they were holding her. Her food was delivered via a door which always closed as quickly as it opened. She gritted her teeth. She could go mad in this room.

There was nothing to take her mind off her situation.

Her only companion was a cobbled-together bed, consisting a couple of old pallets and a rotting mattress. The sheets were in a better state, though badly in need of a wash. There was nothing else in the windowless room, save for a tray containing dried-up, half-eaten sandwiches and an empty water bottle. Paint peeled from the walls and, in one corner, an ominous patch of mould spread its webbed fingers, as though to draw her into itself.

Yes, she had wanted to disappear for a while, but not like this. This was way off the chart. Her parents had wanted her to do well in school, do A-Levels and go to university. Instead, aged fifteen, she had runaway and was living in a communal house with other runaways. Her well-heeled parents had angered her, believing *they* always knew best. Perhaps, they had after all.

4

BLOOD FORENSICS

Yvonne tucked her pen behind her ear and sat back in her chair, a pensive look tensing her muscles, her blonde hair unusually mussed.

Dewi came into the office, smiling, his chest puffed out. "Got some names to check out for the burglaries in Bettws. Seems like a solid tip."

The DI looked up at him, her awareness of her surroundings returning. Bettws, a small village, six miles from Newtown, had recently seen an unfair share of fuel-oil thefts, van break-ins and, most worryingly of all, home break-ins. In at least one of the latter, the occupants were asleep in bed.

Yvonne's face relaxed. "Good work, Dewi. Who are they?"

Dewi proceeded to run through the suspects and their links to the area.

Yvonne nodded. "Great. Ask Callum and Dai to check the whereabouts at the time of the break-ins. The DCI will be cock-a-hoop if we can nail this one."

Dewi tucked the file under his arm. "You were deep in thought, ma'am. Anything you want to share?"

Yvonne rubbed her ear, her eyes narrowing. "I was just thinking about Mrs Jones. Have we had the forensics back on that blood sample from the magazine?"

"Oh yes, I almost forgot. Er, the blood group was B-positive and," he scratched his head, "it was from a male."

The DI looked at him wide-eyed. "Male?" She pursed her lips. "So, not from our girl?"

"I'm afraid, not."

"Well, I didn't expect that."

Dewi shook his head. "No, but it does mean that, if there has been a disappearance of a young girl in the area, we may have the blood of the perp."

"Still nothing reported, then."

"Not a sausage."

"It's very odd. Maybe Mrs Jones really did read too much into things. Having said that, if the girl was a runaway, there may have been no-one to notice she was gone."

Dewi scratched his head. "Well, with next to two-and-a-half thousand people going missing in the UK each year, I'm thinking needle in a haystack."

The DI shrugged. "Keep the results on file. Let's crack on with the burglaries. I may ask Clayton to do a bit of digging in the national misper files. I'd hate to think we let someone down."

5

INCIDENT AT THE FLEA MARKET

Welshpool Cattle Market thronged with all manner of people. One of the biggest flea markets of the year was in full swing. China, books, vinyl and all manner of curios were changing hands at a fair rate, if not always at a fair price. The craggy Shropshire hills served as a romantic backdrop.

Newly-weds Sarah and John had come down to see what they could get for their new home. Sarah really wanted a large chandelier for the dining room, but the usual high street prices were well beyond their reach. She hoped the flea market would have the answer, even if they had to do a little up-cycling.

Something caught her eye. An Art Deco telephone made of pale-green marble and brass. An old-style, circular dialling ring adorned the front. The wires were badly frayed and would need to be replaced, but Sarah thought it beautiful. She pulled John's arm to tell him so. His eyes were firmly fixed elsewhere. She followed his gaze, curious as to what had gripped him so.

A boy, probably no more than twelve or thirteen, was

being carried by three men in dark clothing. The men had their backs to them and were some distance away, heading for the parked cars. The boy struggled to free himself. Sarah couldn't see his face. John made a start towards the men. Sarah looked around to see if anyone else had noticed. John began running and she followed, fumbling for her mobile phone.

A side-door to a large, white transit van was torn open and two of the men clambered in with the boy. The van was muddy and there were no windows, save those in the front cabin. The third man jumped into the driver's seat and fired up the engine. John was still several feet away and panting hard, when the van pulled away, tyres screeching on gravel.

"Shall I call the police?" Sarah shouted to John, waving her mobile in the air.

Another woman joined them, bending over to catch her breath. "What was that?" she asked, hands on hips.

John shook his head. "I don't know."

"I heard the boy crying," the woman wheezed.

The incident had clearly been witnessed by several others. A small crowd had formed.

"Ring the police." John nodded, rubbing the back of his neck. A fine sheen of sweat had gathered on his brow. He took several paces in the direction the van had gone, as though he might catch up with it, but returned, muttering to himself.

Sarah felt a cold, tingling up her sides as she punched nine, nine, nine, into her mobile. She held her breath.

The operator coolly asked her which emergency service she wanted.

"I need the police. Please hurry, we've just witnessed an abduction of a child," Sarah said, the words tripping over themselves.

"Hold the line."

Sarah bit her lip, scraping a shoe along the dirt. As soon as the police call-handler answered, she rapidly related what they had seen. The handler assured her help was on the way.

John watched his wife, still muttering to himself. He held out an arm, his hand motioning her. "Is that the police? Can I speak to them?"

Sarah passed him her phone. Her hand shook so much, she almost dropped it.

John appeared not to notice. He grabbed her mobile and blurted a registration number into it, as though he were a volcano, no longer able to contain the magma churning in his chamber.

Sarah was impressed that he had thought to remember the number. She had not even registered it. She narrowly managed to not throw up.

6

ABDUCTED

The dreaded rattle of keys against the door and turning in the lock, hailed the intrusion of two masked men in black, hooded clothing.

Fourteen-year-old Peter shivered and let out a cry, as they grabbed and dragged him roughly towards the door. Each man placed a hand on the boy's neck, keeping his head bent such that the floor was all he could see. Their fingers hurt, as they dug into his flesh.

They walked quickly, their knees bumping his thighs, his arms twisted to encourage pace. Their stale sweat smelled like urine.

He was taken along a corridor to a room, brightly lit in the centre, with dark corners. When they let him go, he could make out what looked like a large tripod. It carried a movable arm, upon which was a camera.

His shirt was roughly torn from his body and his wrists were bound with a zip tie to his front. They put him on a stool, lit from overhead. The heat beat down on him and he could feel the sweat developing on his chest and back.

The man behind the camera used the arm to move it

above the top of Peter's head. Then, he moved it on down his tear-stained face toward his bound hands. The mechanical arm moved around him, the camera flashlight going off intermittently.

Peter looked for the door, mentally trying to work out how he might get out of the room. But, he was surrounded. There had to be at least six men present, he decided, although some of them inhabited the dark corners and he could not be sure of the exact number. Too many to take on, that was for sure.

"Tilt his head," the cameraman ordered, his voice deep and gruff. "Let's get a good shot of those tears."

Peter steeled himself. If they wanted tears, he wasn't going to give them any more. He jutted out his chin in defiance. His pupils were huge.

"Why are you doing this to me?" he asked, in a high-pitched voice, his chest heaving.

"Pale, dirty and distressed. This is *really* good." The camera man continued panning and tilting.

"You'll go to jail," Peter continued, though he recognised the futility of his words.

"Damn. I need to take that angle again." The camera man peered at his monitor, shaking his head.

More hands on him, moving him this way and that, until the cameraman was happy.

"Right, that's it. We can wrap it up." He moved his tripod back. "I think we have everything we need."

And that was it. Peter was marched back to his room in the same rough manner he had been taken from it. After the door closed, he leaned back against the wall, and sobbed. The tears were of release and relief, that they had done nothing other than film him.

~

"It's very quiet in here, Dewi." Yvonne placed a full mug down for her DS, glancing around CID.

"Thank you." Dewi leaned back in his chair. "Everyone has their head down, ma'am. We're close to nailing this burglary team."

Yvonne nodded. "They've done some great work. When this is over, we should get out for an office meal. I'm thinking maybe the Shilam."

"Sounds good."

Dai Clayton put down his telephone and fast-paced over to them, his cheeks unusually ruddy.

"Is everything okay?" Yvonne narrowed her eyes, searching his face.

"Ma'am, we've had a report of an abduction of a young boy from Welshpool." Dai spoke quickly, his eyes darting from Yvonne to Dewi and back. "Uniform have headed out that way."

Yvonne put both her hands behind her head, whilst Dewi sat bolt-upright.

"Give me some detail." The DI took her hands down and reached for her pen.

"The boy was estimated to be twelve to thirteen and was witnessed being bundled into a van at the Welshpool flea market."

"Witnesses?"

"Several, ma'am. Including a couple who got the van's registration number."

"Details of the van?"

"They're running the reg number now, ma'am. Should have the details any minute."

"What about the boy?"

"Not much known about him, yet."

"Who was he with?"

"We don't know. No-one has reported him missing."

Yvonne and Dewi exchanged glances.

The DI ran over to grab her coat from the back of her chair. "Let's get over there and find out what's going on. I'd like the chance to talk to the witnesses. This isn't the first time this week we've been informed of a potential abduction. What is going on?"

Dai's desk phone rang again and he ran to answer it, frowning as he spoke.

"What was that?" Yvonne asked, buttoning her coat and grabbing her bag.

Dai cleared his throat. "The van reg, ma'am. It's a ghost vehicle. It's registered to person who has been dead for three years."

Yvonne rubbed her chin whilst that fact sunk in. "False plates. If these *are* actual abductions, they're evidently planned. Come on," she said, finally. "Let's go and talk to the witnesses."

THE MARKET WAS STILL GOING, although it was beginning to wind down. The queues in the metal cattle stalls had dwindled. Some of the stall-holders were beginning to pack away their wares.

John, Sarah and a few other witnesses were huddled near to the car park, holding enamel mugs of tea that a few kind stall holders had supplied.

Yvonne and Dewi waited patiently for them to finish giving their statements to a constable. As the PC left, Dewi asked him if copies of his notebook could be sent up to CID. The PC nodded.

John put an arm around his partner, as they related what they had seen to Yvonne and Dewi.

"Did you get a look at the men?" Yvonne asked John.

John shook his head. "No. I saw them from behind. I can only tell you that they wore dark clothing and hooded tops. They were wearing their hoods up. I ran as fast as I could but they had bundled him in and had driven away before I could get there. I just concentrated on remembering the registration and getting that to you. It's all I could do."

"Did you hear any names called out?" Dewi asked.

"No, none."

"What convinced you this was an abduction?"

John pulled a face. "Well, the way the boy was lifted and carried. I'm sure he was struggling. The men seemed to have difficulty holding him."

"But, you *were* some distance away."

John nodded. "I was. I couldn't see their faces. I didn't see the boy's face, either. But, I *am* positive he did not want to be taken into that van."

"Thank you." Yvonne smiled at John and Sarah. "It was very quick thinking of you to get the van's number and we are very grateful to you for that. You did everything you could. Now, it is down to us to find out who that boy is, why he was taken, and get him back home to his family. We may need to see you at the station at some point. Would that be okay?"

John nodded. "Of course."

Yvonne turned to look at the car park. They were very close to the Welshpool bypass. The van could have been on the main road out of the area within five minutes. And could have been travelling north or south.

"We'll request all the local CCTV," Dewi reassured, reading her mind.

"What is going on, Dewi? What is going on?" Yvonne rubbed the base of her neck.

"I don't know." Dewi sighed. "But, I've a feeling we are going to find out."

7

MISPERS

Yvonne was scribbling, head down, when the DCI came to see her.

"Ah, I thought I'd find you here. How are you? Everything okay?"

She was about to answer, but he continued and she closed her mouth again.

"Control have been in touch. A young girl has gone missing from Llanidloes. Name of Donna Fitzpatrick. She didn't return home after attending the Cefn Lea christian conference place above Dolfor."

Yvonne sat bolt upright, eyes shining. "Did you say above Dolfor?"

"Yes, why? Ring any bells?"

"As a matter of fact, sir, it does. A Mrs Jones in Dolfor reported the disappearance of a young girl who she said had been waiting at the bus stop at Dolfor."

"Yes, I remember. Well then, check it out. Find out if the descriptions match up." He ran a hand through his tousled hair.

"Will do, sir."

THE FIFTEEN-MILE DRIVE to the town of Llanidloes took around twenty minutes. Yvonne and Dewi would speak to Donna's friends first, and then head to Cefn Lea. Perhaps, they might have some answers.

As they drove over the bridge in Llanidloes, the DI was reminded of the beauty of this part of Wales. The first time she had visited the place, Dewi had informed her that it had been at the heart of the medical kingdom of Arwystli. The impressive Cambrian mountains provided the backdrop. Like Newtown, it nestled around the banks of the River Severn.

They arrived at the three-storey, terraced black-and-white house where Donna and her friends had been living. They had left their car in the town car park, by the river.

Their knock on the viridian-painted front door brought them face-to-face with a tall, slim, sullen-faced young man. Yvonne estimated him to be around twenty-five years old. She held up her ID.

"DI Giles, and this is DS Hughes. May we come in and speak with you? I understand you contacted us about a missing girl."

"Oh, yeah. That's right." He took gum out of his mouth and held it in his hand, standing back to allow them through.

They passed into a decent-sized kitchen via the narrow hallway. The male motioned them to the chairs around a square table.

"Was it yourself who reported Donna missing?" Yvonne asked, whilst Dewi took out his notebook.

"No. It was Lisa, her friend." The young male didn't sit, but rather stood, leaning against the kitchen cabinets. He was dressed in a dark, hooded top and jeans, darkened by ingrained dirt, and the top had food stains down the front. He kept his hands in the front pocket of his top, shifting position every few seconds. His eyes darted around, as though he was expecting something to happen.

"Could we take your name?" The DI's voice was soft and low.

He hesitated, looking out through the window.

"Joe. Joe Benton."

"Thank you. Is Lisa here, Joe?"

He shook his head. "She's out. She'll be back later."

"Can I ask how old you are?"

His eyes darted to her face. "Just turned twenty-eight. Look, this isn't about me-"

"Is this place rented?"

"Yes." He sighed and folded his arms.

"Whose name is on the tenancy?"

"Mine." He glowered at her. "Look, what's that got to do with Donna going missing?"

Yvonne pursed her lips, looking down at the table. "I understand you're worried. Please tell us what you can about Donna and what happened."

"She was supposed to be back last Friday."

"Is that from Cefn Lea?"

"Yeah. She was into all that stuff."

"Religion?"

"Yeah."

"And she didn't come back?"

"No. She texted Lisa to say she was on her way, but she never arrived."

"Do you have access to a vehicle, Joe?"

"Yes."

"Can I ask what car you've got?"

"It's a Peugeot." He looked through the window again.

"Is that the black one parked outside?"

He nodded.

"Do you have Donna's mobile number?"

"No." He looked away again. "Lisa has it. But, it's switched off. Goes straight to voicemail when you try ringing it."

"Do you have a photograph of her? A recent one, if possible?"

He shook his head. "She's got a Facebook page. Donna Fitzpatrick. You'll be able to see her on that. Nobody keeps paper photos anymore." He looked at her with one eyebrow raised, a look designed to tell her she should know that already.

"How old is Donna?" Yvonne stared directly at him and he averted his gaze.

"Not sure. Sixteen, I think."

"We have a possible witness to her disappearance."

His wide eyes darted once more to her face.

"The witness seems to think that she looked around fourteen."

He shrugged and shifted position. "Maybe."

"When did Donna begin living here?"

"Mm, dunno. About four months ago."

"Where was she from?"

"Birmingham, I think."

"How did she end up here?"

He tutted and moved to the window. "She didn't like where she was living, okay? Kids chat online. Someone told her about this place."

"And that you'd take her in if she came here?"

"I don't turn anyone way, do I?"

"Do you work, Mr Benton?"

He had his back to her now. "Of course. I couldn't pay the rent otherwise."

"What do you do?"

"I work in Tescos."

"Newtown?"

"Yeah. I'm on night shifts at the moment. I should be sleeping now."

"How long have you been working there?"

"Since I dropped out of... Three years."

Yvonne stared at him intently, her eyes narrowing. "You went to college?"

"Yes."

"But you dropped out?" She said it with a gentle voice.

"It's not what you think. I got my degree. I was working for my PhD, when I gave up. It wasn't for me. I was doing it for my family."

"Is that when you came to live here?"

"I want to live *my* life *my* way."

Yvonne nodded. "How many people are staying here, Mr Benton?"

"That depends."

Yvonne raised her eyebrows. "On what?"

"On how many people need a roof. Not more than seven or eight though, usually."

"Are there others here at the moment?"

"Sure. There's a few upstairs in the rooms."

"Do you mind if my sergeant goes to speak with them?"

He shrugged. "Whatever."

"Thank you."

Yvonne nodded towards Dewi, who rose from his seat to head upstairs.

The sound of a key turning in the front-door lock set Benton tapping his fingers on the countertop.

The DI could see that he was on edge. She said nothing.

The kitchen door was pushed open by a dark-haired, petite young girl, who looked around fifteen. She stopped when she saw the detective sitting at the kitchen table. She set two shopping bags down on the floor and pushed wayward hair from her face with a shaking hand, looking up at Benton. His face was impassive.

"This is Lisa," he offered, turning to fill a glass with water from the tap.

"Lisa." Yvonne nodded the greeting and gave her what she hoped was a reassuring smile. "I'm Yvonne Giles. Police. I understand your friend is missing."

Lisa nodded and pulled out a chair from under the table. She took off her khaki bomber jacket and draped it over the back, before sitting.

"Have you found her?" Lisa's wide eyes darted around the DI's face.

Yvonne shook her head. "Sadly, not. Though we may have had a sighting. Do you have access to Donna's Facebook photos?"

Yvonne was acutely aware of Benton still leaning against the kitchen cupboards. Lisa repeatedly looked up in his direction.

"Yes. Yes, I do. Would you like to see her profile picture?"

"Yes, please. Is her profile public?"

"Yes."

"That's great. We need as recent an image as possible, if we are to jog people's memories and get their help in locating her."

Lisa passed her mobile to the detective.

The picture was of a smiling blonde-haired girl, striking a devil-may-care pose. Her face full of life.

"And this is recent?"

Lisa nodded. "Taken two weeks ago, down by the river.'

"Can I ask how old you two are?"

Lisa coloured. "Fifteen."

"And Donna fifteen."

"Nearly."

"So, she's still fourteen at the moment."

"Yeah, that's right."

"Where are your families?"

"My family are in Newport." She shook her head. "If you can call them family."

"What about Donna?"

"Hereford, I think. She said her mum lives near the cathedral. I don't know about her father. I think he left when she was tiny. She spent some time in care. Her mother had an alcohol problem."

"Lisa, how did you come to be living here?"

Lisa flicked another look towards Benton.

Yvonne felt intense irritation at his continued presence, and it surprised her.

"I needed my own space."

The DI rubbed her chin. "You're fifteen-"

"Things were difficult at home. I couldn't take it any longer."

Yvonne gave a nod, her expression soft. "What about Donna?"

"I think she wants adventure."

"She's a free spirit," Benton chimed in.

"I see. When was the last time you heard from her?"

"She Facebooked me from Cefn Lea. She couldn't text as she had no signal." Lisa grimaced.

"What did she say?"

"That she'd be back with us on Friday."

"And that was last Friday?"

"Yes. She said she was on her way."

"And you've definitely not heard from her since?"

Lisa shook her head. "Nothing."

"Could we have copies of her last messages? And photographs if possible?"

"Yes. No problem."

"Thank you, Lisa... and Joe." Yvonne made to get up.

"Will you be coming here again?" Benton's hands were on his hips.

"It's possible, yes." Yvonne turned back to him. "In fact, I'd say it's quite likely. Will that be a problem?"

It was a full two seconds before he replied with a shrug. "Guess not. Just call us, first. Best make sure someone will be here."

As Yvonne moved through the hallway, she met Dewi coming back down the stairs.

"All done," he assured her.

They thanked Lisa again, as she accompanied them to the door. The DI put a hand on her arm. "We will do everything we can to find your friend."

Back at the station, Yvonne filled Dewi in with what she had gathered from Lisa. Likewise, he told her about Sally and Martin, the two youngsters he had spoken to in the rooms upstairs.

"Martin said he was sixteen and Sally, fourteen." Dewi frowned. "Joe Benton is definitely the man in charge. I can't say that he's doing anything untoward, but it's very unusual to have a twenty-eight-year-old with a bunch of teenagers living in the same house."

"I agree." Yvonne tapped her pen against her lips. "I think, perhaps, we should have a word with social services. Find out if they are aware of those youngsters living there. I bet they are all on misper lists. Get Callum onto that, would you?"

"Yes, ma'am. Will do."

Dai Clayton came up to the DI's desk, pen behind his ear and both shirt sleeves rolled up to his elbows. The hair around his face appeared damp.

"Everything okay, Dai?" she asked, her face creasing into a frown.

"Just had a call from the Jenkins family in Meifod. They haven't heard from their son, Kyle, in two days. They thought he was staying with a friend but the friend's parents claim they have not seen him and Kyle's friend reckons he lost Kyle at the flea market and assumed he'd changed his mind and gone home."

Yvonne sat upright. "Our missing boy."

"Could be. Seems likely."

"Let's cross-check his photo with the description John and Sarah gave us. Better still, go see them and show them Kyle's photograph. See if they can confirm that he's the boy they saw."

"Will do, ma'am."

"Oh, and Callum? Ask the family if Kyle had been talking to anyone online. We may need to borrow his computer and any other devices, for a while."

"Yes, ma'am."

8

MAKING PLANS

That evening, Yvonne kicked off her shoes and padded through to the kitchen. The coldness of the hard flooring penetrated her stockinged feet and was somehow both comforting and relaxing. A cooling balm, which travelled the length of her.

She made a ham and tomato sandwich, with more than its fair share of thick mayonnaise, and tucked in. Images of children being taken from the street swirled in front of her. Children she had never met, but who haunted her as if they were her own. She put down her half-eaten sandwich and walked to the window.

The wind moaned out in the dark and rain wended itself in perpetual streams down the window. Little rivers, that changed direction with the every gust. She stood mesmerised, in a tired, trance-like state, until her landline jolted her out of it.

Her heart thudded against her ribs. "Yvonne Giles."

"Hey... it's me." Her sister Kim's familiar voice was very welcome at that moment. She couldn't have timed it better.

"Hi, Kim. It's good to hear from you."

"Are you okay? You sound different. Have you been running?"

"No." Yvonne smiled into the phone. "The phone made me jump is all."

Kim laughed and Yvonne could hear her nephew and niece in the background.

"Yvonne, there's a big event coming up next month and we want in on it."

"Really?" A frown creased the DI's forehead. "What event is that? Do I know of it? I'm not sure what you mean."

"The big one?"

"Er..." Yvonne wrinkled her nose. "No, you're going to have to tell me, it's too cryptic. Need another clue."

Kim gave a belly laugh and Yvonne knew at this point that she must be being really thick.

"I give up. Put me out of my misery, *please*."

"The big four-oh!" Kim sounded incredulous at her sister needing to be told.

"Oh, my word, you're right. I had forgotten. How on earth could I do that?"

"Anyway," Kim laughed again. "What have you got planned and can we gate crash? I'd been meaning to organise a surprise, but it's been manic here and you're been very hard to pin down."

"It's fine, sis. I hadn't thought about it at all. It's been really busy at work. But, now that you mention it, there is no-one I would rather spend my birthday with than you and those gorgeous children of yours."

"We could come to you?"

"Great idea. I will get the spare room ready for you and maybe we can catch a movie with the children and take them to an all-you-can-eat Chinese."

"Sounds fabulous. We could be with you on the Saturday morning and even fit in a birthday lunch."

"Even better, and it's just what I need." Yvonne really did feel lifted by the thought of it, momentarily forgetting her worry over the missing youngsters.

She was still smiling when she climbed the stairs to bed. But, her dreams were filled with desperate attempts to save children.

∼

"Yvonne, can you come and see me in my office?" DCI LLewellyn smiled, but his eyes were glazed, as though his mind was elsewhere.

She followed him down the corridor, breaking into a run in an effort to keep up.

He closed his door behind them. "I want everyone together tomorrow morning for a briefing on the abductions of Donna Fitzpatrick and Kyle Jenkins. I'd like people to bring any information they have. We need a strategy."

"We've issued APB's for both children, but we're going to struggle to find the vehicle involved in Kyle's abduction."

"I heard it's a ghost vehicle?"

"That's right, sir. They used the details of someone who's been dead for three years."

"Obviously well-planned."

"Absolutely."

"What's the word on the street? Are we looking at a pedophile ring?"

"Can't say at the moment, but we're looking into whether either of the victims were being groomed online. I have to say, though, so far, we have found no evidence of that. Nothing untoward on their tablets or mobile phones."

"So, we don't know how they were chosen?"

"All we can say for sure is that the kidnappers might have assumed that children *would* be present at the flea market. The abduction of Donna is an odd one, though. I mean, who could have predicted she'd have been at that bus stop at that time? Her abduction looks to be opportunistic."

"Except, her housemates would have known."

"Yes. And I cannot rule out their involvement, yet. I found the living arrangement at the house strange and we've informed social services. Joe Benton would have us believe he's a bleeding heart. But, he's a twenty-eight year old living with very young teens. I found him a little creepy."

"Can you check his computers?" Llewellyn tilted his head to one side.

"Yes. I've been wondering if Donna could have been picked up by the same van as Kyle. Perhaps it was on it's way to Welshpool for the flea market and just came across Donna on the way. They picked her up because they could. The Jenkinses described a side-opening door on the van. Would have been a very quick pick-up, which might explain why Mrs Jones missed it. The only thing is, the van was registered to an empty flat in Aberystwyth."

"Yes, it's all very odd. But, we've got to keep on it. The community is feeling extremely nervous. Just check out the news tonight. So much pressure." He sighed.

"I will, sir."

She ran her eyes over his tousled hair and his shirt coming out of his trousers. "Are you all right, sir?"

"Yeah, fine. I'll leave it with you."

She was dismissed. She shrugged and got back to it.

9

WALLS

It sounded like a scratch, at first. A scratch that became a definite knocking. Faint, but audible. It sounded like it was coming from the heating pipes.

Donna climbed off her pallet bed and crawled along the cold, tiled floor to bend her ear to the pipes. She listened for several seconds before calling, with her cheek to the cold, rusty metal, "Hello? Hello? Can you hear me?"

She listened. Holding her breath. Biting her lip.

A scraping sound vibrated the pipe against her ear. She heard a muffled, male voice. She thought she heard excitement in the hesitant words.

"Hello? Who's there?"

"Donna. My name is Donna. Who are you? I've been kidnapped and brought here against my will. Can you help get me out of here?"

"I'm Peter. Did you say you've been kidnapped, too?" He sounded less hesitant.

"Yes. Does that mean you are a prisoner here, too?"

"I am. I was beginning to think I was on my own." Peter

had a coughing fit and Donna momentarily removed her ear from the pipes, giving it a rub.

"Are you all right in there?" she enquired, as soon as her head was back in position.

"It's cold. There's no heating in here."

"Nor in here." Donna shifted position as her back ached.

"Do you know what they want with us?"

"No. I guess you don't either?"

"They were making some sort of movie and taking pictures of me." Peter's voice shook.

"Did you say they were filming you?" Donna asked, still struggling to hear.

"Yes."

"What sort of film? Are they pedophiles?" Donna swallowed hard, her heart thudding. She had to get out of here.

"I don't know. They didn't touch me. They were just filming. Looked like professional kit."

"Did you say they looked like professionals?"

"Yeah."

Donna heard footsteps in the corridor outside.

"Peter? I've got to go. I'll be back later." She ran back to her bed and sat on the edge, breathing hard. She clenched her fists, her eyes fixed in a glower, towards her door.

THE SOUND of keys turning in the lock echoed in her room. Her stomach sank and she felt an urgent need to defecate.

"I need the toilet." She skewered the intruders with her stare, her pupils so large they made her eyes look black.

"You're not gunna be any trouble, are you?"

She was grabbed roughly by one of the masked men, who twisted her arm up behind her back.

She squealed in pain.

"You'd better be quick," he spat. "We have important work for you."

She gulped. Her throat was so dry, it hurt. There were no more words. She was half-pushed, half-dragged along the corridor to a small cubicle, which she was rammed into. They kept the door open.

"Shut the door," she said in a hoarse voice and, when they didn't respond, added a reluctant, "please."

She might just as well have not bothered. They did not shut the door. However, she need not have worried. They talked in hushed tones amongst themselves, not paying her any particular attention. This left her both relieved and afraid. What did they *really* want of her?

Having cleared her bowels, she continued her rough journey down the corridor. A masked man either side of her, keeping her head facing the floor. She got a sense that there was at least one window to her right, as there was daylight on the corridor floor. If only she could turn her head, she might be able to identify a landmark. No such luck. Their hold was like steel.

"What took you?"

She could hear the harshness in the voice. Whoever was waiting for them was not impressed.

"Well, she's here now. Let's just get on with it."

Head still to the floor, she tried to identify which of the voices was dominant. She might need that knowledge. She couldn't decide.

"Camera ready," another voice called out.

One of the voices had a strong Welsh lilt. The others? She wasn't sure they had an accent. Or, if they did, they hid it well. That struck her as unusual. She still couldn't place where she might be. She had guesstimated the journey in the van to be around an hour. But, that could put her in either England or Wales. Everywhere was easily accessible from the border.

"Get up there."

She was pushed towards a stool and her head was let go. The harsh studio light stung her eyes and she blinked numerous times, as she attempted to get onto the stool which was a little high for her.

One of the men gave her a push up. Once there, she was aware of the thick menace of their presence around the room, though she could not quite see them. The man worked the camera on a long, articulated arm. He weaved it in and out of the light. He, too, was masked. They had been careful not to use names, yet each man appeared aware of his role. They were well coordinated.

That they might be terrorists crossed her mind and her stomach sank again. She wondered if this was a pre-emption of her beheading, or some other insane act.

"Head up."

The order rang out like a gunshot and she jumped, her heart smashing the blood relentlessly through itself. She felt faint and thought at any moment that she might throw up.

"Turn your head to the left... Now the right."

Out of left field, a hand clashed against her jaw. She screamed, her own hand flying to cradle the hurt. Hot tears coursed down her cheeks.

"Good." The cameraman continued to move the camera in and around. "This is *very* good. *Exactly* what I wanted to capture."

At that moment, her tears dried up. If it was tears they wanted, she would make sure they didn't get any. Her jaw throbbed, but she jutted it out. "My friends will cut your balls off."

One of them laughed. Not a real laugh. A lingered,

disdainful cackle designed to wither her spirit. Her hair was pulled from behind with such force, the back of her head was almost horizontal with the floor. Her throat, fully exposed. She swallowed painfully, praying for it to be over.

"Got the blood?" the cameraman enquired.

A figure came out of the shadows, smearing metallic-smelling liquid onto her cheeks.

She pulled her fist back, thrusting it out in an attempt to connect with the smearer's head. He ducked, and her arm was once again twisted up painfully behind her back. She cried out.

"Great. Great work." The cameraman was in his element.

When her arm was let go, she hunched over, drained. She no longer cared what the cameraman was doing. She wanted to curl into a corner, alone.

Ten minutes later, she got her wish. They threw her into her room, tossing a packet of sandwiches and a plastic water bottle after her. She placed her head in her hands and softly sobbed.

10

GHOST

The sun shone out of a near-perfect sky. Her breath created cotton wool clouds around her head. She turned to Dewi, who was humming to himself. From their position, on the road leading to towards the Aberystwyth seafront, she could see a tiny triangle of ocean, through a gap in the houses at the front. They had parked their car on double-yellows. The DI placed her 'police emergency' card on the dash, before locking the doors.

"Under different circumstances, this day would be beautiful." She sighed, staying for a moment to purposely savour the cold, salty air.

"It *is* beautiful." Dewi winked at her. "The circumstances are bad, but the day? It's beautiful."

She admired that. Admired his ability to always see the positive. He had that ability to lift her spirits when things appeared bleak.

She took her canister of mace out of her bag and placed it in her pocket.

Dewi looked at it and pulled a face. "Oh, no." He grinned and took a couple of steps away.

She laughed back, as she remembered the time he had surprised her on a stake-out in Chester, and she had maced him in the face. "Last time served you right. Don't creep up on me, is all. Whistle or something."

He exaggerated a tut and turned his back to her, in an affected manner.

It had done the trick. She *did* feel more relaxed. Not a bad thing, under the circumstances.

They were outside the address where the ghost van was registered. Uniformed officers had already searched the property and found nothing. They had decided that the address was completely unconnected to the van or its drivers.

Yvonne wanted to speak to the landlord. Make up her own mind. Why *had* the abductors used this address, one of a block of student flats in Aberystwyth? She did not really believe in coincidences.

The flats were owned by a professor at the college. An IT specialist, who rented them out to students. Dr. Carl Carantan was on her list of persons of interest. He joined Joe Benton, the housemate of Donna Fitzpatrick.

They had agreed to meet the professor at the empty flat.

Dewi rang the bell, repeating the action and pursing his lips when the door was not opened in a hurry.

Carl Carantan had wild, red hair, flecked with mousey blonde. Thirty-five to forty years old, he appeared confident and clean-shaven. He moved with a feline efficiency, backing up in a gliding motion, as he beckoned them in. Yvonne took him in. Jeans with a tweed jacket, over a red-check shirt. His eyebrows were almost as wild as his hair. Unusual, in one still relatively young.

"Doctor Carl Carantan?" Yvonne asked, though she knew it must be he.

"Carl, please." He signalled for them to take a seat on a pale-cream, leather sofa, in the open plan lounge-diner. Kitchen worktops ran along the length of the farthest wall. The place was semi-furnished, ready for potential new occupants. Light poured in from unfettered windows.

"French?" Yvonne would not usually use words so sparingly, but with him, it felt like the right thing to do.

"English," he corrected. "My father was French. My mother, English. I was born in Gloucester and grew up in Wallingford."

The DI's eyes widened. "Wallingford? That's not far from Oxford."

"Correct. You know it?"

"I lived in the area for several years."

He nodded. "How can I help you?" he asked, directly.

The DI answered just as directly. "This address was used to register a vehicle which we believe was involved in the abduction of a young boy."

"I know." He scratched his head. "Some officers came here yesterday, wanting to search the place. I told them it's been empty for several weeks. The new tenants won't be here 'til next month."

"Who were the last tenants?" Dewi crossed his legs at the ankles, as he took notes.

"A student couple. Chinese. The boy's name was Kwok Chai. I'm not sure of his partner's name. He was the one who dealt with me and completed the paperwork."

"Have they been back to the flat since they cleared out?"

"Not at all. They were in the flat for their final year. They stayed a few months after they graduated while they spent some time exploring the country. They returned the keys the day they left and that was the last I heard from them. As far as I know, they have returned to China."

"I see." Yvonne tapped her pen against her lips. "Do you come here regularly?"

"I come here occasionally for maintenance purposes. I wouldn't say it was that regular."

"Do you live in Aberystwyth?"

"No. I have a house in Talybont, near Cwm Einion."

"Artists Valley?" Dewi acknowledged. "It's pretty there."

"It *is* beautiful," Carantan agreed.

"Do you have a vehicle?" Yvonne straightened a little, to ease the discomfort growing in the small of her back.

"I do. I drive a black BMW." He eyed her, coolly.

The DI was unfazed. "Do you have access to a white Transit van?"

Carantan sighed, placing both hands on his hips. "There's something you need to get straight. I have not abducted a young boy. Neither, would I. That's what you came here for, isn't it? You think I might be somehow involved. That's an utterly ridiculous notion and, if you were not carrying that badge of yours, I wouldn't even grace it with an answer. I would have nothing to gain and everything to lose from doing such a thing."

"I'm sorry." Yvonne's eyes softened. "This is our job. If it were your child who had been taken, you would want us to leave no stone unturned."

He opened his mouth and closed it again, staring hard at the coffee table.

The DI continued. "The name used to register the vehicle was Mathew Hinds."

He shot her a look from under half-lidded eyes, as though he didn't want her to see into them.

"Did you know Mathew?" she asked, giving him a couple of seconds before continuing. "He is said to have killed himself three years ago, jumping off Constitution Hill."

"I knew him as well as I know any student." He said the words slowly, his guard still in place.

Yvonne got the distinct impression that he was holding back.

"Did they find out why he killed himself?" She leaned forward towards Carantan.

Carantan shrugged. "As far as I am aware, the pressure had gotten to him. His father was a strict disciplinarian and Mathew had felt as though he would never be good enough. His grades were slipping and he couldn't deal with it and didn't want to face his father."

"But, that brings us back to how, and why, the men who took Kyle Jenkins used the details of a dead Aberystwyth student. And, an Aberystwyth address to register their vehicle. I strongly believe they must have a connection to the town, if not the college."

He brushed non-existent fluff from his trouser legs. "I've no idea," was all he said.

∼

As they left the block of flats, Yvonne gave an involuntary shudder. She had the feeling someone had walked over her grave. She was glad of Dewi's company, she was feeling out of sorts.

Dewi paused beside the car. "Ma'am, would it be all right if I had a walk through town? It's Carol's birthday and I'd like to take something home."

Yvonne snapped out of her reverie. "Oh, gosh, yes, Yes, of course. Please tell her happy birthday from me."

"I will." He smiled. "I've booked a meal for her, tonight. It's a surprise. I thought I'd buy her a new dress to wear."

"Dewi, that is such a wonderful idea. She will be

thrilled. Yes, please go on into town. I can meet back up with you in a couple of hours. I have a friend I am hoping to meet for lunch, so that will work out well."

They agreed to meet mid-afternoon, giving them both ample time to do their own thing for lunch. Yvonne phoned Tasha.

As she placed her phone back in her handbag, a young man, around twenty-years-old, came running out of the block of flats. Yvonne watched him go to a battered Ford and root around the back of it.

She walked towards him. He hadn't seen her yet. He puffed and sighed heavily, running both hands through his hair, as though upset at losing something he'd expected to find in the car.

Yvonne cleared her throat. "Are you okay?"

He jumped, taking a moment to switch focus from whatever it was he was worrying about.

"Yeah fine." He sighed. "Sorry, do I know you?"

She shook her head, taking in his striking blue eyes and shoulder-length fair hair. His white t-shirt hugged a toned frame.

"You live in the block of flats over there?" she asked, flicking her head in their direction.

"Yep. I live on the top floor. Name's Mike." He narrowed his eyes. "You come to see the empty flat?"

"As a matter of fact, yes." It wasn't a lie.

He looked her over. "You're not a stud-"

"No, not a student. I've just been talking to Dr. Carantan." She stopped there.

He looked her over, as though examining her motives.

"I wondered why he was over." Mike leaned his hand on

the roof of the Ford. "He'll be very happy that someone is finally moving in."

She opened her mouth to correct him, but closed it again.

"More rent, you know?" Mike added.

"I guess Dr. Carantan doesn't come over here that often, then."

He shook his head. "Not in the daylight, anyway."

She raised her eyebrows.

"He works long hours." Mike gave a shrug, but looked uncomfortable. "If he comes out to check on the building, it's usually pretty late." He rubbed his palms on his thighs. "Anyway, I'd better go. See you, if you move in." He gave her a cursory wave and jogged back to the flats, leaving Yvonne wondering what had made him so nervous.

～

THEY HAD AGREED to meet by the chip shop on the main promenade. Yvonne had to admit that she was starving and Tasha's idea of fish and chips by the sea really appealed. The nip in the air lingered, but, as long as the sun remained out, it was pleasant enough. Spring approached.

Tasha hugged her friend tightly and insisted on buying the food.

Yvonne was too hungry to argue and, food in hand, they ran to the beach-front, to sit on the wall and dangle their legs above the sand.

The cold air, though sapping the heat from their food, failed to dampen their enjoyment of the salty, comforting potato-ness of it. There was a freedom in these times. The DI could almost forget the stress and worry of her day-to-day. Almost.

Tasha finished her food first. Screwing up her chip paper, she gave her friend a broad smile and, seeing Yvonne was not yet finished with hers, set off running to the nearest public bin to post her rubbish ball.

The DI watched her and felt a pang-like regret, of something found and lost to her. She turned her gaze back to the ocean, seeking solace in its calm bathing of the shoreline.

"What's troubling you?" Tasha was back and regarding her, with narrowed eyes.

Yvonne shook her head. "I wouldn't know where to start."

"What are you working on?" Tasha probed, tilting her head to one side, as though to see underneath the hair that had partially hidden her friend's face.

The DI knew those dark eyes were seeing right through to her core and she sighed. The next moment, she was pouring her heart out about the case. Bringing the psychologist up to speed with what they knew and, just as importantly, what they did not.

"Do you think the children were abducted by a paedophile ring?" Tasha asked, chewing her cheek as she mulled over the information.

"Maybe, but that doesn't exactly line up. I mean, pedophile rings are usually pretty secretive. Abducting kids in broad daylight, in a public place, is generally not their scene." Yvonne screwed up her face. "It's almost as though this gang *knew* they would be observed and *wanted* to be."

"But, you said they registered their van to a false address and used a dead person's details."

"They did. This was very well-planned. It's like they want people to know that abductions are taking place, but not who is doing them."

"Like shadows."

"Exactly."

"Terrorists?"

"Unlikely. They would surely have announced they had done it by now, or demanded some sort of ransom. Nothing has been announced by the kidnappers. Not *so* far, anyway."

"So, it's their move next," Tasha said, turning her gaze to the ocean.

"It seems like it." Yvonne sighed. "It won't stop me trying to chase them down. We don't have the resources to stake out every public function in Dyfed Powys. However, we may be able to cover some of the biggest. And, that is what I am seriously considering. I have a feeling, though, that the DCI may not like the plan. We'll see."

11

VORTEX

To Yvonne's utter disappointment, Welshpool town CCTV and the bypass CCTV had been non-operational for some time. She was crestfallen.

"I'm really sorry, ma'am." Dewi put a hand on her arm. "A cost-cutting measure. The council told me it may be reinstated soon, but they are making no promises."

Yvonne shook her head. "What is the use of having these things if we're not using them? Now, we have no way of knowing where Kyle's kidnappers took off to. For all we know they may be in England." Cheeks puffed right out, she let out a lungful of air.

"The van is almost certainly being kept in a lock-up or garage, somewhere. We've had officers, all over, keeping an eye out and... not a sausage."

"We're shooting in the dark." Yvonne's eyes glazed as she mulled things over.

"Ma'am, you need to see this," Dai Clayton shouted from the other side of the office. He was with Callum Jones and they were staring down at Callum's laptop, on which they were watching the lunchtime BBC news.

Yvonne and Dewi rushed over. There, in front of them, was a screenshot of a Facebook post, showing a young male, bound and clearly in distress. The accompanying words left them staring, open-mouthed. The DI felt a cold chill spread upwards from the base of her spine. The post was styled like a 'Go Fund Me' post. But, this was far more sinister.

The newscasters reported the comments, which had been left by an outraged public, and outlined how the message had gone viral within thirty minutes of being posted.

"Dai, Callum, can you get it up on Facebook? Let's get a proper look at it," Yvonne instructed, eyes still on the news bulletin. "Use another laptop. I want to see the whole of this broadcast."

The post was trending on both Facebook and Twitter.

Dewi read the words, aloud. 'Peter needs YOUR help. He is suffering in isolation, away from his family and friends. He will be tortured and killed, unless we can raise one million pounds in Bitcoin to save him and others like him. You will see photographs of others soon. Head over to YouTube to see our videos. Remember, we need to raise one million pounds in Bitcoin. Payment details to follow.'

It had been posted by a group calling themselves 'Vortex.' A search on YouTube brought up a bunch of videos featuring men in black clothing and hoods, wearing white, goateed masks identical to those worn by the group calling themselves 'Anonymous'.

Dewi leaned on Callum's desk. "Are they an offshoot of the hacker group? Or something else?"

Callum shook his head. "Anonymous have issued a statement denying all knowledge of Vortex."

"Vortexes. Tornadoes and whirlpools. Destructive forces." Yvonne pursed her lips. "So they want Bitcoin? I was wondering if this sort of thing would happen eventually. The possible consequences of having a dark web and unregulated currencies."

The BBC news bulletin continued. A family had come forward to say that the fourteen-year-old boy featured in the post was their son Peter. He had run away from their home in Machynlleth, Powys, some three weeks before. They could find no trace of him.

The presenters went on to say that the prime minister had called an urgent meeting and would be issuing a statement, as soon as they could verify if the threat was real.

"We have to assume the threat is real." Yvonne sighed. "It would be neglectful to do anything else. I'm guessing the intelligence agencies will be all over this one. MI5, GCHQ and SOCA."

Dewi put a hand on her shoulder. "Well, we were here first, and we won't be muscled out. They will need our help."

~

THE NEWS MEDIA was full of the Vortex story and little else. DCI Llewellyn's forehead was shiny, as he ran a hand through his hair and paced his room. He hadn't heard Yvonne's light tap on his door. She pushed it open and cleared her throat, noisily.

"Yvonne. Come in." He stopped pacing and turned to her, lips pressed into a thin line.

"You wanted to see me?" She looked at him, eyes wide.

"Yes. I've had the chief super on the blower. A couple of officers from SOCA are on their way to speak to us. They are especially interested in the van used to snatch Kyle Jenkins and will be chasing down that lead.

Yvonne frowned. "What if Kyle's abduction isn't linked?"

"Looks like they are working on the premise that it is. If we handle this correctly, these guys could be a great help to us, whether or not our disappearances are linked."

"I see." Yvonne folded her arms, leaning back against his office door, her eyes flicking from side-to-side as she mulled it over. "When will SOCA get here?"

"We're expecting them later today. I'd appreciate it if yourself and Dewi could be with me when I talk to them."

"Of course."

"They'll want to talk to the couple from Welshpool. They may be the only people to have seen a snatch team in action."

"That can be arranged, sir."

"What about Mrs Jones at Dolfor? Can you talk to her, again, and ask if she remembers any vans going past. See if she has remembered anything else that might be useful to us."

"I can get up there this afternoon, that's no problem."

"Thank you, Yvonne." Llewellyn pointed to the front page of The Times, which lay on his desk. "The PM has ordered that no-one is to pay the ransom, under any circumstances."

Yvonne sighed. "How are they going to police that? If transactions are going through the dark web, how are they going to know? There are a lot of people out there who care. We're talking about youngsters. Hell, people are probably already paying."

"I think you're right. Nonetheless, that is the official line and you should pass that along to the local families, if it turns out that their loved ones have been taken by this group."

The DI closed her eyes, knowing how she would feel if it were a member of her family. "Can't we have an official announcement? Do I have to deliver this, personally?"

"An announcement is too cold and less likely to be adhered to. You and your officers can explain that paying will only encourage this group to take more children." He rubbed the side of his face and the DI could hear the scrape of stubble. He continued, "You know that's right."

Yvonne nodded, her eyes glazed. Her heart weighed heavy in her chest, as she made her way back to her team.

∼

KYLE HAD CRIED himself to sleep for two nights in a row. He had not eaten. He did not want to eat. He wanted his mum and dad.

On the second night, he had told himself firmly that, when he awoke the next morning, all this would be gone. He would wake up in his own bed, to the sound of his mum gently knocking on his bedroom door, the smell of breakfast wafting through to him. The crisps, sandwiches, bottles of coke and the pop-up tent, would still be in the cupboard with the electricity meter, where he and his neighbourhood friends had left them. He would return them all to his friends. Running away had seemed like a big adventure. He would be the neighbourhood daredevil, earning him huge respect from the other kids. The whole thing had been a stupid idea. What he needed now was to feel his mum's arms around him and smell the warm, faint perfume of her shampoo.

When he was taken along the corridor to the filming room, surrounded by monsters, there were no tears. He was all cried out. But, his body shook. Under the spotlight's glare, he cried out for his mum and his dad. Though the tears had dried up, the evidence of their passing was woven through the dirt on his face.

12

SOCA

Yvonne picked up her grey trench coat and made for the door. "I'm off to see Mrs Jones in Dolfor. I'll probably be about an hour," she said to Dewi, on her way out.

"Would you like me to come with you?" He made to follow her.

She turned back, briefly. "It's okay, Dewi. I'm sure Mrs Jones won't bite me. I'll be fine by myself. What I would like you to do, however, is chase up the blood spot we found on the magazine. Find out if the DNA cross-checks with any DNA on file. You never know, it could be the jackpot."

"Will do, ma'am." Dewi held the door open for her. "Don't get distracted by anyone dangerous." He grinned.

"Oi, less of your cheek." Yvonne grinned back. "I'll have my Mace with me." She held up the can to him and grinned exaggeratedly. He backed off in mock horror.

∾

MRS JONES HAD MADE a pot of tea, in anticipation of the DI's arrival, the latter having phoned her to check the visit would be okay. The older woman was dressed more casually today, in blue jeans and a cream jumper. The clothes still managed to look smart on her thin frame.

Yvonne, on the other hand, had thrown on her attire that morning. She had grabbed a white, cotton blouse which, though clean, had not been ironed, and a tartan skirt. She was still wearing her coat when she sat down.

Mrs Jones handed her a cup and saucer, eyeing the DI's mac as though unsure whether she should offer to take it.

Yvonne accepted the tea, placing down the saucer and holding the cup in both hands, appreciating the warmth.

She blew on the hot liquid. "Mrs Jones, I've brought photographs of a girl I'd like you to see. Would it be all right for me to get them out?"

"Photographs? Of course. Are they photographs of the girl I saw in the village the other day?"

Yvonne nodded. "We believe they might be. But, I'd like you to take a thorough look and, if it is not her or you are not sure, tell me."

The DI leaned over the small, oak coffee table and spread the few photographs which Donna's friend, Lisa, had supplied from social media.

Mrs Jones took her time, looking over each one carefully, before finally pulling back.

"It's her." She tapped one of the photographs emphatically. "And, those are the clothes she was wearing, when I saw her."

"Her name is Donna Fitzpatrick." Yvonne looked into the older lady's clear blue eyes. "We believe she was waiting for a bus to take her back to Llanidloes. A bus that would have gone via Newtown."

Mrs Jones slowly shook her head. "And, she didn't get there?"

"No. She didn't get there. Her friends reported her missing a couple of days later. You were probably the last person to see her, besides her abductors."

"Oh." Mrs Jones twirled a handkerchief around in her fingers. Yvonne noticed dark shadows under her widened eyes.

"I wanted to ask you if there is anything else you remember from that day? Anything, no matter how insignificant it might have seemed?"

"Well, I... No. I don't think so?" At that moment, Mrs Jones' Welsh accent sounded more pronounced.

"What about the vehicles?"

Mrs Jones shook her head. "I didn't see any vehicles."

"I know. Did any of the sounds stand out to you? Anything about any of the engines, that might indicate the type of vehicle?"

Mrs Jones leaned forward, shaking her head.

Yvonne was about to thank her for the tea and gather the photographs, when Sheila narrowed her eyes.

"No, wait. There *was* something. My knees were hurting, and I was rearranging the cushion under them."

"Go on."

"I heard what could have been a side door on a van opening. The engine noise was soft, but probably a van."

"You didn't remember this before?"

"I guess I tuned it out. Vehicles sometimes stop in the lay-by. I didn't hear a disturbance. No struggle. But then, I guess I wasn't listening for one at the time."

"We've spoken to your neighbours, Mrs Jones, and no-one else saw Donna. We're very grateful for you calling us. It is people like yourself that help us solve many crimes.

Thank you." Yvonne rose from her seat, a soft smile lightening her face.

"Oh, it's the least I could do. That poor girl." Sheila Jones' mouth curled downwards. "I hope you find her soon and that she's unharmed."

When Yvonne returned to the station, two men in suits were with the DCI, who was showing them around CID.

Llewellyn smiled broadly and let out a relieved puff of air, when Yvonne strode in.

"Ah, Yvonne, come and meet George Lucas and Mark Lyons, a DI and DS with SOCA. George, Mark, this is DI Yvonne Giles."

The senior of the two men held out his hand for Yvonne to shake. She did so, meeting his relaxed and confident gaze with one of her own. George Lucas looked to be in his mid-fifties. Hair thinning on top, he disguised a burgeoning middle-aged spread with an oversized suit jacket. He had a well-lined, but kindly face. She mused to herself that his retirement probably was not that far away.

His companion also stepped forward to shake her hand. About twenty years younger, Mark Lyons appeared to keenly observe what was going on around him. His head would fly round at the slightest sound. He had the air of someone who constantly expects something to happen.

"George and Mark are here to familiarise themselves with what's been happening." Llewellyn flicked his head towards the window. "As regards the missing children."

"Welcome. Pleased to meet you both," Yvonne murmured, resisting her strong urge to courtesy. Exactly how *did* one communicate with members of SOCA. "You know we have witnesses to the abductions. Two who saw a boy taken, and one who saw a girl, just before she was taken." Her gaze was cool and level. It belied her nervousness.

George Lucas nodded. "We'll need to talk with them as soon as possible. Can you arrange it?"

"Sure. Unfortunately, we don't have CCTV." Yvonne pursed her lips.

"We know." Lucas looked round at LLewellyn, and back again. We were just discussing that."

"We're locked in a battle with the council to have our CCTV reinstated." Yvonne added, "Cost cutting, of all things."

"We know that, too. And, unfortunately, so do the kidnappers."

Yvonne eyes snapped up to Lucas'. "What?"

"We think that is how they are deciding where to hunt."

"They know which councils are not operating their CCTV?" Both her eyebrows were raised in surprise.

"Whoever this organisation is, they are *very* computer savvy."

Yvonne rubbed her chin. "We've had officers out combing the car park in Welshpool, from which Kyle Jenkins was abducted. They found nothing. They are not just computer savvy, they are extremely careful not to leave any trace of themselves."

"*And* they are operating on the dark web," Lyons chimed in, "making it very difficult to trace them or their transactions."

"I thought that would be the remit of MI5?" Llewellyn placed both hands in his pockets. "Isn't that *their* territory?"

Lyons puffed out his chest. "Oh, we do our fair share of digging around in there, believe me. But, so far, nothing."

"So, where do we fit in?" Yvonne asked. "I'm guessing you won't want us involved in the web stuff?"

"That's right." Lucas perched on the edge of the desk, folding his arms. "But, you may be able to help pinpoint the local snatch team. If we can identify one of the individuals, we'll have a way in. Of course, we can't act until we can identify them all and take them all down at the same time. We couldn't risk leaving anyone behind."

"Or, harming the hostages." Yvonne's eyes narrowed. "We have to remember these are children. They will be terrified and they're relying on us to help them. We can't let them down."

"Best not get *too* involved, emotionally," Lyons suggested.

Yvonne felt patronised. She put both hands on her hips. "Well, if that's all, I've got work to do."

Llewellyn nodded his consent and she left the room, concerned that her team's effort could be stifled by the SOCA invaders. She mentally chastised herself for the thought.

13

PLAN OF ACTION

Yvonne poured herself a coffee, rolled her sleeves up, and sat at her PC, notebook and pen at the ready. She relished the peace and quiet, now that the rest of her team had headed home. She had stayed on to do some research. The quiet was just what she needed.

The kidnappers were demanding Bitcoin in exchange for the release of the hostages. She had heard of the cryptocurrency, but that was about it.

She placed her pen in her mouth and opened Google. Wikipedia was as good a place to start as any.

She scribbled fast, sitting back every once in a while to read through her summary. It took over an hour for her to truly get the gist of what it was about.

It had been devised as a currency of the people, for the people. A decentralised, unregulated way for money to change hands without the need for banks or other financial institutions. Transactions were verified by ordinary computers all around the globe, which kept the system incredibly accurate. What Yvonne wanted to know was how it could be so easily used by the underworld to hide their nefarious transactions.

If she had understood correctly, it was because it was possible to generate a new Bitcoin address for each transaction and a multitude of such addresses could be accessed by a single password. Bitcoin millionaires had been created in their hundreds in the last ten years and it seemed that governments had only just woken up to smell the coffee. Only now were they beginning to wonder whether they should legislate and regulate.

She sat back in her chair, tapping her pen on her teeth, deep in thought. The sound of a throat clearing, behind her, had her jumping out of her seat, hand to her chest.

"Chris!" It shot out like an accusation. "How long have you been standing there?"

He smiled. "Oh, I dunno. About five minutes?"

"I didn't realise you were still here." Her face softened. "You startled me."

"So, I see." He grinned. "Anyone would think you were up to no good."

"If I wasn't so tired, I'd throw something at you." She pouted at him. "I thought I'd do some digging minus the distractions of a busy office. What are you still doing here, anyway?"

Llewellyn lifted both hands to the back of his neck. "I've been wading through the bumf that's come down from the top. They really want a tight lid on the information flow around these abduction cases."

"Do they have a handle on Vortex?"

Llewellyn walked over to perch on a desk next to the window. "No. Everyone, and I *mean* everyone, is on the case. SOCA, MI5, MI6, the Home Office, and I'm sure the chief super said the FBI are helping in an advisory capacity. I'm told it's being treated as a terror attack."

"Wait, aren't the public being told this is nothing to do with terrorism?"

"I think that is to avoid misinterpretation. They don't believe this *is* anything to do with extremism. They think its pure financial opportunism. But, Vortex do appear to be operating in cells."

"I see."

"Anyway, information will be strictly on a need-to-know basis, and I would appreciate it if you would run stuff past me before discussing it with anyone else."

"What about the team?"

"Tell them information is to stay within these walls. Any doubts, come and talk to me."

Yvonne nodded. "I think I'm all wrapped here. You about ready to go?"

He shook his head. "Not quite. You go. I won't be that far behind."

⁓

THE FOLLOWING MORNING, Yvonne could feel a developing dampness in the small of her back, as she prepared to take the lead in the team briefing. Perhaps, she was coming down with something, her throat *did* feel scratchy. She hoped there were no wet patches in the back of her blouse. She scribbled a few notes on the board, while everyone filed in. She wasted no time on lead-ins.

"Okay, listen up. SOCA have been in touch, to say that the council are reinstating CCTV, but only those at top level will be made aware. The public are to remain oblivious of the change, meaning we cannot use CCTV evidence for any other local crimes. This news is to stay in this office. Am I making that clear?"

There were murmurs and nodded assent from around the room.

"How did SOCA manage to wangle that?" Dewi pulled a face. "We've been on at the council for days."

The DI shrugged. "Power, Dewi. SOCA have it and *we*, evidently, don't. Anyway, a lot of the instruction will have been coming from the very top."

"What, the PM?"

"The Cabinet Office and the Home Office."

"Do you think Vortex will target our area, again?" Callum raised his right eyebrow, arms folded across his chest.

Yvonne turned to face him. "No-one can say for sure whether the group are looking for more victims. However, the intelligence agencies believe that there's a high likelihood that, if they do, they will look at the areas they know. The areas *they* believe are soft touches."

"And, we have a smaller police force and, as far as they are concerned, poor CCTV coverage." Dewi scratched his head. "So, how do we stop them picking off our youngsters?"

Yvonne turned back to the whiteboard. Her hand moved swiftly, as she noted the main points.

"This group appear to be snatching from major, public events. Places where there will be a lot of people and a lot of vehicles. Places with a lot of potential victims and where the abductors won't stand out. We know they are using ghost vehicles and any suspect regs can be run through the system pretty quickly."

"Are you suggesting that we stake out all the public events in the area?" Dewi placed his hands on the top of his head. "We don't have that kind of manpower."

"I know." Yvonne nodded. "That's not what I'm suggesting. Look, the intelligence services will be hunting this group online, trying to trace dark web transactions and any other communications. They will also be coordinating any attempts at rescue. That won't be our bag. But, where we *can* be of use, is in locating our local snatch team or snatch teams. We can't stake out every big event or venue. We can, however, stake out the biggest and most public. I say we do what I suspect *they* are doing. We scour the local media for what's coming up and we choose what we think would be a good target."

"Ma'am, are we talking weeks? Months?" Callum's forehead was deeply furrowed.

Yvonne tilted her head, her eyes, soft. "You worrying about the overtime, Callum?"

"Well, I-" He shifted in his chair, his movements stiff.

Yvonne cast her gaze around all the officers in the room. "Because, it *will* be necessary to put in extra hours. Your family time *will* be disrupted. I'll try to make sure it's divided up as evenly as I can, and we may be able to get a few regular officers, in plain clothes, to help us out. I can reassure you that I will be trying to shoulder as much of the burden as I can. But, it goes without saying, it's going to take more than me to stake out an event. It also goes without saying that, however put out we may feel, there are victims and their families out there, going through far worse. It is for those that I intend to bust my gut." She pursed her lips.

Callum nodded. "I'm up for it, ma'am," he assured her.

She beamed her thanks, as everyone else offered there assurances that they were in. Her team was pure gold.

14

DETERIORATION

Her door swung open with a loud thud, jolting her out of a fitful sleep. The room was too dark to properly make the men out, there being no window in her room, and she was sure night had fallen. The corridor outside was dimly lit. The surprise had set her nerves on edge and her heart pumping so hard, she could hear it in her ears.

"Up. Up. Up." One of the men grabbed her by the arm, yanking her from the bed.

She found her tongue. "Get off me." She tried pulling her arm away, but ended up with both arms restrained. "I want a phone call. Let me call my parents-"

"Shut your mouth!" The man who ordered this shoved her in the back. She would have gone over were it not for her restrained arms.

"Take off your masks, cowards. Let me see your faces." She spat at one of them.

They did not reply. They continued to half-push, half-drag her along the corridor.

Someone was fighting, coming out of the room next to hers.

"Peter?" She called out to him and was rewarded by having her head pushed down, so far that she was bent almost double. She could see her knees.

"Donn-" A muffled reply from the boy who, it was clear, was faring no better.

"Where are you taking us? Where are you taking us?" She could barely walk in the position they were holding her. Searing pain ran through her back.

"Get in there," one of the men growled, as both she and Peter were thrown to the floor in the room.

"That boy hasn't eaten anything. Get him to eat." That was the final order, before the men disappeared again, keys locking the door.

At least there was a small amount of natural light coming into this room, supplied by a tiny skylight. Scudding clouds rippled over a half-moon.

"Are you okay?" Peter asked her.

She held a hand out to him and he squeezed it. Her attention was already focussed on a small boy, hugging his knees, rocking himself backward and forward. He appeared not to notice them.

Donna felt great sadness at seeing the young boy in such a state. He reminded her of her brother. She sat next to him, placing an arm around his shoulder. Not too tight. She chose not to say anything, but rocked backward and forward, matching his rhythm.

At first, the boy paid her no heed but, after a while, he leaned his head on her shoulder and the rocking slowed.

Donna held a hand out to Peter, who had sat on the edge of the bed next to them. She wanted him to know she had not forgotten him. He rubbed her shoulder.

The younger boy let out a tiny sob and Donna pulled back enough to look at his face. She placed a hand either side of his head.

"Honey, we're here," she said in a half-whisper. "See? We're here."

"Mom?" he asked, though she was not sure if he was speaking to her.

"No, honey, I'm sorry. I'm not your mom." She brushed the hair back from his eyes. "I'm Donna. What's your name?"

He continued looking straight ahead, as though dazed.

"Is your name Brian?" she prompted.

He shook his head.

"Kevin?"

He shook his head, more vigorously this time.

"Iggle Piggle." It was the only CBeebies character she could remember.

"No, silly." She thought she caught a tiny smile, just before his face became guarded once more.

She placed the palm of her hand on the boy's forehead. It felt hot. She was sure he was running a temperature. She said so to Peter.

"I found some water." Peter handed her a plastic bottle, approximately half-full.

She twisted off the cap and sniffed it, before placing it to the boy's lips.

He took a sip and she let out the breath she'd been holding.

"It's Kyle," the boy said, in a voice she could barely hear.

"Kyle," Donna repeated. She looked around at Peter. "His name is Kyle."

"Hello, Kyle." Peter reached out to touch Kyle's arm. "I'm Peter, and I'm very pleased to meet you." His voice shook and Donna realised that he was shivering. He was bare-chested.

She took off the full-sleeved, cotton blouse she was wearing over a t-shirt, and put it around Peter's shoulders.

"Thank you," he whispered, and put his arms into the sleeves.

Donna continued to cuddle Kyle. They were no longer rocking. She gave him another sip of water. "Will you eat for us, Kyle?"

He shook his head.

A paper plate lay next to the bed, on which were sandwiches which had not yet gone dry. Donna broke off a small piece and held it to Kyle's lips. He turned his head away.

"He's not gunna to want to eat if he's got a temperature." Peter ran a hand through his close-cropped hair and strode over to the door, giving it a resounding kick.

Donna felt Kyle jump in her arms.

"Peter," she whispered, "please."

"Sorry." Peter came back to the bed. "Who are these nut cases? What do they want? We've got to get out of here." His voice still shook, a little.

"Come sit with us," she said, her voice soft. She held out an arm.

He paused, as though torn between wanting to tear the room apart and wanting the human closeness. He chose the latter, holding the other two tightly. They sat like that for an age, until they felt the pull of sleep. Donna took off one of her socks and sniffed it, before pouring a little water onto it. She placed it on Kyle's forehead, as she lay him down.

He put a hand to it, repositioning it a little, and closed his eyes. Donna lay next to him. Peter lay down the other side of Kyle, an arm draped loosely over the younger boy and Donna.

A WELL-DESERVED GLASS of chardonnay in hand, Yvonne switched on the evening news. Her wood-burner threw dancing shadows around the room. She stood with her back to it, soaking up the warmth.

As expected, the headlines were dominated by the burgeoning story of Vortex and their diabolical demands. It seemed that every commentator in the country wanted to have their say. And, they were being joined by commentators from a good many other countries. It was hard separating fact from noise, or even downright propaganda.

The bulletin switched to newsreel of the prime minister meeting families of the hostages. The DI could see, even in brevity of the images, the darkness below the premier's eyes. Her hunched shoulders betrayed the magnitude of the burden for which she was ultimately responsible.

The shot changed to one of her at a podium, outside of 10 Downing Street. Her gaze resolute, she ordered her countrymen and women *not* to fulfil the Vortex's demands for Bitcoin. Just as with terrorists, she stated, to pay them would be to encourage the taking of more hostages.

Back in the studio, they stated that some Bitcoin mining companies believed that many ordinary people had already begun paying some of the Bitcoin ransom. They thought they had detected a surge in transactions.

"I can't say I blame them," Yvonne said out loud. "These are children. Who wouldn't want to help save them? The kidnappers knew exactly what they were doing, going after a such soft target."

UNEXPECTEDLY, their abductors had allowed Donna and Peter to stay in the room with Kyle all night. Donna woke and held her breath, as she extracted herself from the two sleeping boys. For the first time since her abduction, she was not feeling the cold.

She sat bolt-upright in the semi-darkness, blinking, in an attempt to bring the room into sharper focus. Dawn was breaking outside.

She turned to look at the boys. Kyle was sleeping with his head on Peter's chest. Peter's breathing gently stirred strands of the younger boy's hair.

The nerve-jangling sound of keys against the lock and a small tray was pushed in along the floor. The door closed again.

"Wait," Donna whispered, afraid to wake her sleeping companions.

The bringer of the food paid no heed.

Lightly stepping from the bed, she examined the tray. Two packs of sandwiches to share between the three of them and a two-litre bottle of water.

The water was welcome and she poured a tiny amount onto her head, before taking several mouthfuls. She resisted the food. That could wait until her friends woke up. They would all eat together. Perhaps Kyle would eat more if he was sharing it with them. But, if he didn't? She was sure he would need a doctor. He had felt frail in her arms, like someone only barely present. His ribs stuck out like the rungs of the old Victorian radiator that stood in their room. The one that was not working. She was sure his parents would be devastated if they saw him like this.

Peter stirred, she watched him jerk out of his relaxed slumber, sitting bolt-upright, as he remembered his captive state. A frown darkened his handsome features.

"We've got to get out of here." The words hissed like escaping gas from between his teeth.

Donna leaned forward to place a comforting hand on his arm. "Careful," she whispered, her gaze tender, "you will wake Kyle."

He flicked a glance at the younger boy, extracting his leg from where it had been partially trapped beneath him. "I can't stand it anymore." He shook his head, placing a hand on each ear and looking up toward the skylight.

Donna bit her lip, feeling the need to distract him and ease his angst.

"Where are you from, Peter? Where were you taken from?"

Peter took his hands down from his ears, regarding her silently for a few moments. Water shimmered in his eyes, but no tears fell.

"Machynlleth. I ran away from home. I was sick of living with mum and dad and was hanging out with mates. I wanted adventure. I was mad for it. They grabbed me from the park." He flicked his head in the direction of the door and rubbed his forehead. "My mum'll be crying her eyes out."

"You miss her?" Donna asked, walking over to check on Kyle, as he slept.

Peter hung his head, his shoulders hunched. "Yeah, I miss her. I've really messed up."

Donna came back to put her hands on his shoulders. "You were great with Kyle last night. Don't be too hard on yourself."

"What about you?" he asked, giving her no more time on him. "Where you from?"

She sat next to him, leaning back on her hands. "Hereford. I'd run away from home, too. Been living in Wales, in a place called Llanidloes. I was on my way back there when they grabbed me."

"Are we all runaways, here?" He turned to look directly at her. "Is that what this is? Do you think they know?"

Donna shrugged. "I don't know, maybe." Her eyes narrowed. "But, how could they? How could they know?"

He shook his head. "You put anything on Facebook?"

"A little. What about you?"

"Yeah, but my profile and posts are friends-only. Anyway, I'm pretty sure Kyle isn't a runaway."

"What are they after?"

"I don't know, but, I *do* know we need to get out of here."

15

SUSPICIONS

"What's going on?" Yvonne ran down the last tier of stairs to join several uniformed officers in the station lobby. Vehicle sirens cut through the chatter, as they headed out.

"Attempted abduction, ma'am," a female officer called back, adjusting her ear piece.

"Where?"

"Garthowen. Two small boys. We're going to do a sweep and interview them."

"We'll follow on," Yvonne called back, already returning upstairs to find Dewi. She found him drinking a coffee and pulled a face. "Oh, sorry, Dewi. You won't have time to drink that. We've got to go."

Dewi's disappointment was quickly replaced by expectancy. "Ma'am?"

"Attempted abduction on Gathowen."

Dewi needed no further prompting.

~

Parking the car, they could see the throng of officers, parents, children and onlookers.

Yvonne pursed her lips. "We'll have our work cut out."

"Leave it to me, ma'am." Dewi puffed himself up, as he shut the car door. Straightening his jacket, he strode over to the ever-increasing crowd and flashed his badge. A pathway opened up as people moved back, still craning their necks.

A young PC scribbled into his notebook as he asked questions of a man and woman, who stood next to a young boy with a blanket around his shoulders.

Yvonne stepped forward. "May I?" She directed at the officer.

He nodded and flicked his notebook closed.

"Sorry, do you mind taking statements from the other witnesses? I want to talk to the boy and his parents."

A look of exasperation was quickly suppressed. He opened his notebook again.

Yvonne turned to the parents of the young boy. "I'm DI Yvonne GIles. Is there somewhere we can go?"

The female nodded and pointed to a house in the middle of the row facing the road. "We live there. I'm Helen Thomas and this is my husband Jack. Zac is out little boy. He's had a heck of a fright."

Yvonne estimated Helen and Jack to be in their early thirties. "How old is your son, Mrs Thomas?"

"He's eight." Helen Thomas pushed open the gate to their small front garden and led the way down the path. She turned every couple of seconds to check on Zac, who was close behind her. Dewi followed, and Jack Thomas brought up the rear.

There were no flowers in the garden. No frills of any kind. Just grass and a pathway. Simple, but tidy.

Helen pushed open her front door and led them

through the tiny hallway, to her kitchen at the front of the house. She put the kettle on and adjusted the elastic band holding her ponytail.

Jack Thomas held his son, who was still wrapped in the pale-blue blanket.

"Hello, Zac." Yvonne's voice was soft as she sat at the oblong kitchen table. She glanced at Dewi, checking he was ready to get everything down in his notepad. "I heard you had quite a fright."

Zac nodded, pressing himself into his father's stomach.

"Can you tell us what happened?"

The boy looked up at his father, who smiled and squeezed him. "Go on. They're going to find the men who grabbed you."

Zac squirmed, his face reddening.

"How many men were there, Zac?" Yvonne decided simple prompts would be best.

"Two." He shuffled inside the blanket.

"Can you tell me what they looked like?"

He shook his head.

"What colour hair did they have?"

"Brown, I think."

"Okay. What did they do?"

"One of the men grabbed me." The corners of his mouth turned down, as though he was about to cry.

"It's okay, Zac." Yvonne tilted her head. "It must have been frightening." She gave him a moment before continuing. "What was he wearing? Can you remember?"

Zac shook his head.

"What colour was his top? Can you remember that?"

"Green. I think it was green." He nodded for emphasis and was rewarded with a big smile.

"That's brilliant. That is very useful, Zac. Can you remember the colour of his trousers?"

He screwed his face up. "Erm... black? I think."

"Okay. So, you think they were black trousers. Would you say they were definitely dark?"

"Yes." He appeared more sure of that.

Yvonne got off her chair to kneel in front of the boy. "Can you show me how he grabbed you?"

Zac looked up at his father, before taking a step forward and placing a hand on each of the DI's shoulders. His fingers dug in.

"What happened then?"

"Michael shouted at him to get off me."

"Michael? Who is Michael?"

"My friend."

Yvonne glanced at Jack and Helen, her eyebrows raised.

"Michael lives a few doors down. He's nine and was playing with Zac at the time."

Dewi rose from his seat. "I'll see if I can find him." With that, Dewi left.

Yvonne turned back to Zac. "Did the man say anything to you?"

"He said I'd taken his papers. He told me I had to go with him to the police."

"What papers did he mean, Zac?"

"I don't know."

"Did he have a car?"

"A van. He got into a van with the other man."

"What colour was the van, can you remember?"

"White. I think it was white."

Dewi returned with another young boy.

"Michael?" Yvonne asked, as they approached.

The boy nodded.

"How old are you?"

"Nine and a half." He stood tall, hands on hips.

"Did you see what happened?"

He nodded, again. "I saw the man grab Zac. He was pulling him. I shouted at him to stop."

"What did the man look like? Can you remember?"

"He was tall with brown hair. He had a badge on his jumper."

"What colour was his jumper?"

"Green. Dark green, I think."

"I see."

"It had a red thing on it. Kind of like a planet." He rubbed his cheek.

"Where was the planet? Can you draw it for us?"

"I'll get some paper and a pen." Helen squeezed herself past.

"It's okay." Dewi turned the page in his notebook and passed it and his pen to the boy. "You can draw it in here."

MICHAEL TOOK the pen and drew the rough outline of a jumper on the page. On the top left corner he drew what looked like the planet Saturn. "The planet was in red," he said, screwing up his nose. "There were letters underneath. I don't know what those were."

Dewi pursed his lips. "I think I know that logo. " He took the pad back from the boy and redrew the planet with the name SION underneath.

"Does that look like what you saw?"

Michael nodded. "That's what it was."

"What happened when you shouted at the man?" Yvonne asked.

"He went back to the other man who was standing by their van. They both got in and they left drove off."

"Did you see any of the registration number?"

Michael shook his head. "I'm sorry." He hung his head.

"Hey, hey." Yvonne put a gentle hand on his arm. "You did great." She flicked a look to Zac and back. "You both did. We have got a lot to go on and we are going to find and speak to these men and make sure this doesn't happen again, okay?"

Both boys nodded.

"Thank you." Yvonne held out her hand, to Helen and Jack. "You've been very helpful." Then, looking at the two boys, added, "Come down to the station some time and we'll show you around and you can have a sit in the police cars. Would you like that?"

She was awarded with two big smiles.

"Where we headed, Dewi?" Yvonne called, as they ran back to the car.

"We're off to the St. Giles Business Park, ma'am. The other side of town. A tech firm called Sion have their offices there. I'm pretty sure what the boys described was Sion's company sweatshirt."

Yvonne shot into her seat. "Let's go."

Dewi put the blue light on the dash and set off the siren in brief bursts, as they headed down New Road. Even so, it was a slog to get through. Once past the traffic lights, there was more room and Dewi put his foot down.

Passing the St Giles Golf Club, he cut a right into the business park, driving on until he reached the unit that housed Sion's offices. The logo the boys had described was prominently displayed on the company sign.

Dewi pulled into a space marked RESERVED. He turned to give the DI a wink. "Nice of them to keep it for me."

Yvonne grinned.

"Just before we go in..." Dewi's face was serious once more. "The CEO is a Darren Byrne. This is the second or third startup he's had over the years. A few years ago he was prosecuted for attempted fraud and the company he ran, supplying electronic equipment, folded. He made a lot of the older locals unhappy, as they lost the money they'd invested in shares. I think he was bankrupted. Fours years later, and he's back like a bad penny."

The DI pursed her lips. "And the fraud? What was that all about?"

"If I remember rightly, he was claiming that his equipment was capable of a lot more than it actually was. People were paying way over the odds for junk."

"So, the man's got previous." Yvonne placed her hands on her hips, reading the sign out loud. "'Sion. We ARE electronics.'"

"Er, excuse me." A young-ish man in a dark grey suit and red tie frowned at them from the doorway. "I'm afraid you can't park there. The public parking places are across the way." He pointed away from them.

Dewi flashed his warrant card. "DS Dewi Hughes, Dyfed-Powys police. This is DI Giles."

The guy in the suit paused, running a hand through his short, dark hair. He flicked a glance behind him, before turning back to them.

"What do you want?"

Yvonne noted his fists, clenched by his sides. "We'd like to speak with the CEO of Sion. If he's here." She regarded him with a steady gaze, suspecting that she was looking at him.

He shifted position as though unsure of what to say next. "What do you want with him?" He gave her a stern look.

"Come on, Darren. Let us in." Dewi sighed.

Byrne looked around him, as though seeking reassurance from somewhere. "What have I done, now?" He frowned and placed his hands in his trouser pockets.

"We'd just like to ask you a couple of questions if we could. Can we come inside?" Although she would never have said, Yvonne was feeling the chill and her feet and head ached. She suspected she might be coming down with something.

"I don't have to let you in." He scowled.

"Do you have a reason not to?" Her raised pitch betrayed her surprise.

"I'm busy. We've got a lot on."

"Whose space have we taken?" She walked towards him, using her hand to indicate the reserved parking spot.

"My deputy, Carl."

"Is he not here, then?"

"No. He's out negotiating a large order with a client."

"I see."

He indicated for them to follow him, leading them into the office atrium, a light, airy space with over-sized pot-plants and a leather seating area, beyond which was a large and shiny reception bar in red, topped with black granite.

The young woman seated behind it was busy on the telephone. As he passed her, Byrne demanded, "Hold my calls."

"What does Sion do, Mr Byrne?" Yvonne pulled out one of the chairs in front of his glass desk and turned to look through the window at the wooded landscaping at the edge of the grounds. Dewi sat next to her.

"We supply electronic goods and control systems." Byrne sat behind his desk and took a sip from the glass of water resting on it.

Yvonne turned back, to regard his angular features. She noted his chin was crooked, pointing a little to the left. "What sort of electronic goods?"

"Everything from school computer systems to home gaming set-ups and industrial control software. If we don't have it and you need it? We'll get it."

She nodded. "Where were you at half-past-three this afternoon?"

"Half-past-three?" He looked up at the ceiling, screwing his face up

Yvonne shot a glance at Dewi.

"I was out with Carl, delivering posters and brochures to local businesses."

Yvonne cleared her throat. "Which businesses? Where?"

He narrowed his eyes at her, as though weighing up his answer. "A few business on the Mochdre Industrial Estate, Maldwyn Sports Centre, Garthowen newsagents.

"Did you interact with two small boys?" No point in beating about the bush.

"What do you mean, *interact*?" His mouth partially open, the DI could see his clenched teeth.

"Did you grab hold of an eight-year old boy and tell him you were going to take him to the police?"

His eyes stared unblinking at her, his forehead creased in a frown. He chewed the inside of his cheek. "I left some brochures on the top of a wall outside of the shop on Garthowen, while I made a phone call. The kids came and started messing with them. One of them took some."

"So you grabbed him?" Yvonne looked at him wide-eyed. "Couldn't you have just asked him to put them back?"

"I indicated it with my hand, while I was still on the phone. The kid ignored me. He knocked them and a load fell onto the pavement. I was unhappy about it and I let him know it."

"He said you grabbed both of his shoulders and told him you wanted him to go with you to see the police. Bit of an overreaction, wasn't it?"

"Well, I didn't mean it." He placed both his hands out, palms up. "They could see I was on the phone and they took advantage."

"They were eight and nine years old." Yvonne shook her head. "Were you trying to abduct them?"

His face flushed, eyes bulging in their sockets. "What? Of course I wasn't trying to abduct them. I just wanted to scare them."

"Have you heard of Bitcoin?"

"Yes." He shook his head. "Of course, I have. Hasn't everybody?"

"Ever traded in it?"

"As a matter of fact, yes. I'm a modern entrepreneur. What's *that* got to do with anything?" His eyes dared her to continue on this track.

"We may request some of your records."

He leaned back in his chair. "Fill your boots. But, you'll need a warrant."

As they left, Yvonne could see Byrne's reflection in the window. He was straight onto his mobile phone.

∽

LISA'S EYES SPARKLED, her face flushed, knuckles white, as she fought to find the words to throw at him.

Benton looked up from squeezing his tea-bag with the spoon. "Want one?" he asked, trampling roughshod over her obvious emotion.

"What right have you got to go through my stuff? It's not yours. Just because this house is in your name, does not mean you can creep into our rooms whenever you feel like it." She scraped a chair out from under the kitchen table and plonked herself on it. "What were you looking for?"

Benton finished pouring his milk and joined her at the table. "What makes you think it was me?"

"Well, it was, wasn't it? You've done it before. Donna told me you went through her things."

"When did she tell you that?" Benton looked nonplussed, casually taking a sip of his tea.

"Goddamnit! Why do you always answer a question with another question?" She placed her elbows on the table and her head in her hands, mussing her hair in frustration.

"I think I should wait for you to calm down." He made as though to rise from the table again.

"A couple of weeks before she vanished, Donna told me you went through her things. She thought it was because she had dated you. I told her just because she'd dated you, didn't give you the right to go through her stuff. And, you don't even put anything back the way you found it. That's what gives you away. You have no respect for other people's things."

He shrugged. "I don't remember going through Donna's things, but, if I did, it was probably because she borrowed something and I went to get it back. Anyway, we weren't really dating. I'm too old for her she knew that."

Lisa scowled at him, shaking her head. "What about me?

I haven't borrowed anything from you. What's your excuse with me?"

"Someone said you might be using drugs."

"What? Who? What?" Lisa screwed up her face, shaking her head. "I'm not using drugs. I've had the odd drag at mate's houses but I don't *use* use. I don't bring stuff home."

He shrugged again. "I heard a rumour and I thought I'd better check. You know we'd lose the tenancy if the place was raided. It's a small town. A close-knit community. The neighbours talk."

She folded her arms across her chest. "I don't believe you. What were you looking for?"

Benton gulped back his tea. "You've got a locked suitcase in your room."

Lisa tilted her head, her eyes widening. "So? What's that got to do with anything?"

"I was just wondering what was in it?"

"Is that what you were looking for? A key? You won't find it."

Benton sighed. "Why are you so angry with me? It's like you're blaming me for Donna's disappearance, or something."

"You see?" Lisa slapped her hand down on the table. "You don't take responsibility.

You basically admit to spying on me and you're not even apologising. You're just turning it all back on me, as though it's all my fault. You're always creeping around. Either that, or you're on your computer all day. What do you even *do* on that thing? You're so clever but you waste it all."

Benton pulled a face, picking at a hole in his black t-shirt, his unwashed hair falling into his eyes. "Are you planning on leaving?" he asked, eventually.

"I can't." Lisa shook her head. "Not til Donna gets back. I

can't just abandon her."

"I miss her too, you know." He exhaled through pursed lips, puffing out both his cheeks. "It's not the same here without her. We're all at each others' throats."

As though to illustrate the point, loud music thundered down from the room

above. Benton shot up and strode to the hall, looking up the stairs.

"Turn that bloody music down, will you? We can't hear ourselves think."

The volume upstairs halved. Benton sighed, and took his empty mug to the sink, placing it on the side.

Lisa frowned at it. "I'm not going to wash that up for you."

Benton kicked at the cupboard, and began swilling the mug, giving it a cursory squib of washing up liquid and a swish with the dish brush.

"Happy?" he asked, his face contorted. He looked as though he would really like to hurt her. "I'm off."

He pushed past her and Lisa heard the front door bang on its catch. She put her head back in her hands and cried.

∽

CARANTAN CHECKED both ways along the road, as he left the block of flats. Movements unusually stiff, he lifted the box and carried it to the car. Though the air was chill, he could feel the sheen of perspiration under his arms and down his lower back. He looked up at the window. Curtains drawn. He wet his lips and hoisted the box into the boot.

He flicked through a few songs on the CD and switched it off. He hated them all. He drove the rest of the twelve miles to his home in silence.

The porch lights should have felt welcoming. Instead, he was sweating nervously. With a deep exhalation, he grabbed his briefcase from the passenger footwell and locked the car. Marian would still be up, binge-watching one of her soaps, no doubt. He scowled in the darkness.

Marian was not watching soaps. She was half-way through a glass of red wine and standing in their thirty-thousand-pound kitchen. The half-finished bottle on the counter, suggested this glass was not the first. She must have been running earlier in the evening. Her blonde hair in a loose ponytail, she still wore her jog pants and vest-top.

She looked up at the clock and back at her husband.

Carantan set down his briefcase and loosened his tie. "I'm tired, Marian."

His wife bit her lip, turning away so he would not see the tear escaping down her cheek. She placed the glass on the countertop with a trembling hand. "It's nearly ten o'clock." Her voice was soft, almost a whisper, but he could make out every word.

"We have a lot on." He shrugged. "We're working on something... It's complicated."

"Were you *really* working?" She turned back to him, eyes half-lidded.

His own eyes stared at the floor, flicking form side-to-side. "Did you ring my office?"

He didn't look up. "I was way too busy to answer. It's not the sort of work you can pause. You lose momentum." He thought about the box in the car. It felt like a millstone. Could she see how much his heart was pounding?

She downed the rest of her wine, placing the empty glass in the sink. "I'm going to bed." As she passed, she did not look at him.

He spent the night on the corner-suite.

16

VIRAL

Dai Clayton almost knocked over his chair, in his haste to get the DI's attention. "Ma'am, you need to see this."

Yvonne put down her papers and shot over to his desk, quickly followed by Dewi.

"What is it? What have you got?" She peered over Clayton's shoulder at the image on his screen and gasped. "Oh my god." A blonde-haired girl peered up from below bright lights, her face dry and bloodied. "That's Donna. That's Donna Fitzgerald." The DI leaned over to get a closer look.

"What does it say?" Dewi wasn't wearing his reading glasses.

"It's signed, 'Vortex'. And they're demanding Bitcoin in exchange for her life." She closed her eyes, running both hands through her hair.

"Another Go-Fund-Me." Dewi sighed. "Damn them."

"Except it's not a real go-fund-me." Dai straightened up. "Oh, it looks very similar, but it's a clever mock-up. The real website must be spitting feathers."

"Can't they get it closed down?" Dewi shook his head. "What are they waiting for?"

"They can't." Yvonne perched on the end of Dai's desk. "They close those adverts down and SOCA lose a vital connection to the kidnappers. They have to play along. They have no choice."

She stared back at the photograph on the Facebook ad. Though clearly distressed, there was a defiance on those pale-blue eyes and jutting chin. No doubt, that defiance was the reason for the blood spot they had found on the magazine. This was a girl with real fire in her gut. The DI silently prayed that that fire would not get Donna Fitzgerald killed.

"Get copies of this sent off for enhancement. Let's see if we can pull something or someone out from the shadows."

"On it, ma'am." Clayton's fingers rapidly tapped his keyboard.

Yvonne turned to Dewi. "SOCA and MI5 will be all over this, but it doesn't hurt to do a little research of our own. While Clayton gets on with that, let's go make the coffees. I think I've come up with a way forward for us."

Dewi followed her to the rest area.

She filled the percolator with water. "We know that the van used to abduct Kyle Jenkins, and quite possibly Donna Fitzgerald, was a ghost vehicle registered to the deceased Mathew Hinds."

"Ahuh," Dewi agreed, placing the mugs on the counter.

"The flat it was registered to was a flat in Aberystwyth where Mathew was a student, and where he died."

Dewi turned to look at her.

Her forehead furrowed in concentration. "I think Vortex, or someone within Vortex, knew Mathew, personally."

Dewi screwed his face up, tilting his head.

"No, wait. Hear me out." Yvonne flicked on the switch

and pulled out a chair. "I've been looking him up. Mathew Hinds was a post-doctoral research assistant, newly qualified, when he died. Now, here's the thing." Her eyes sparkled. "He was working at the university, in the Computer Sciences department. In news articles following his death, his parents stated he was excited about his work and proud of his PhD thesis. They said he had planned to continue in the same line of research."

Dewi leaned back in his chair, listening intently.

"I'll show you the articles, later." She scratched her head. "His parents could not accept that he had taken his own life. They fought to get the inquest reopened. Although the first hearing ruled probable suicide, the *second* hearing changed this to an open verdict."

"Did they give a reason?"

"Not that I could find in the articles I could access online. However, we could get a hold of the coroner's report."

"We certainly could." Dewi nodded. "Also, I'm pretty sure the university keeps copies of all their research theses."

Yvonne grinned. "We're on the same page. I looked that up too. It's the Hugh Owen library and I think we should get up there, today, and get a hold of Mathew's thesis. Find out what he was working on. I'll ask Callum to get a hold of the coroner's report."

"We're gunna be busy." Dewi narrowed his eyes. "Can we just have this coffee, first?"

Yvonne grinned and pulled a face. "Let's make it quick."

17

A MYSTERIOUS DEATH

The Hugh Owen library was situated on Aberystwyth University's Penglais campus. A phone call confirmed they had permission for access to Mathew's thesis, provided they show some ID when they arrived.

The two detectives headed up to E floor with the precious book, which the helpful librarian had dug out for them. She said they could use one of the two Carrel rooms available, as it was presently vacant. They just needed to take in an extra chair.

"You know, we probably could have just requested a copy." Dewi commented, a little out of puff after the stairs.

Yvonne gazed across at the views from the windows, which stretched right over the town, to the sea. The students seated at the desks had their heads down. She guessed they must be so used to seeing such sights, they no longer paused to watch. "I like to put myself into a place." The DI tilted her head. "*Feel* what the victim may have felt. See the things they saw. It helps understand them a little better."

Dewi smiled, and took an extra chair from the main

room and followed the DI into the Carrel room. Yvonne placed the precious thesis on the table.

For a few moments, they simply stared at it. Each, in their own way, paying silent homage to the young man who had made such a promising start and had lost his life off a cliff. A young man whose work, they hoped, would bring ideas, if not answers.

The title read, 'Cryptocurrency, Algorithms and the Potential for Criminal Activity.'

Dewi's lips pressed into a tight line, as he pushed the tome towards the DI.

Her fingers were gentle, almost reverent, as she teased open the introductory pages.

"'To my parents, with love.'" She read the dedication aloud. "And my thanks to Dr. Carl Carantan, whose guidance has been invaluable during this process."

"Doesn't sound like someone about to top himself," Dewi murmured.

The DI had deep furrows along her forehead. "He was researching cryptocurrency and in connection with criminal use. If someone did harm him, perhaps it was due to something he had uncovered, or something he knew." She tapped her pen on her open palm. "We have a rogue group, kidnapping children and demanding ransom in Bitcoin. At least one of their snatch vehicles is registered to this dead, young man. And he was working with Carantan and researching cryptocurrency and crime. Did he uncover something that put him in danger?"

Dewi rubbed his stubble. "Mathew, in the same department as Carantan, who owns the flats to which our ghost vehicle is registered."

Yvonne nodded. "It feels like too many coincidences. I'd like to speak to Carl Carantan again."

They flicked through the pages of graphs, explanations and conclusions. There was a whole chapter on the dark web. The DI took several pictures with her mobile of bits she wanted to peruse later.

∽

As they were about to leave the library, Yvonne noticed the fair-haired, well-muscled, young man she had met the day she went to see Carantan. He was examining his own reflection in one of the large windows.

About to duck out, she could feel the embarrassment rising up her face and neck. When he spotted her, he rose from his seat.

"Dewi, can you wait for me at the car?" Yvonne flicked her DS an apologetic look. "Sorry."

Dewi looked across at the approaching lad and raised his eyebrows.

Yvonne pulled a face and Dewi grinned, before doing as he had been asked.

The DI took a deep breath. "Hi." She held out her hand as confidently as she could. "Mike, isn't it?"

"You remembered." He gave her an open-mouthed smile, full of flouride-white teeth. "Mike Jones. And you are?" He shook her hand firmly.

"Yvonne. Yvonne Giles." She retracted her hand and placed it on the handle of her shoulder bag.

He screwed his eyes up. "Did you decide to rent the flat? What are you doing here?"

"I came to look at this." She held up Mathew Hind's thesis.

Mike stared at it, before his eyes went back to her face. "Why did you want to read someone's thesis? And, someone who is no longer here." He shook his head, as though confused and horrified at the same time.

Yvonne sighed, crossing her arms over the book, which she now held to her chest. "I'm going to level with you, Mike. I'm a police officer."

His pupils widened and he opened his mouth, as though to say something. Nothing come out.

"Did you know Mathew Hinds? Did you ever meet him?"

Mike nodded. "I knew him, briefly. I met him when I was doing my third year undergraduate project with Carantan's research group. Look, this isn't really the place for a conversation. Can we go for coffee?"

"Sure." Yvonne thought of Dewi waiting in the car. "I can't be long though. We have a lot on."

"Fine. We'll nip over to the Arts Centre. They do a great coffee there and we'll be able to talk."

Once seated, with a stunning view over the town to the sea, Yvonne blew on her latte and waited for Mike to finish examining his own reflection, again, and elaborate.

"My project was part of my degree course, contributing a sizeable portion towards the final degree mark. Mathew was in his first year as post-doc."

"Post-doc? So he already had a PhD?"

"Yes, and he was employed as a post-doctoral research assistant. He was effectively in charge of seeing me through my project. Of course, we had guidance from Carantan. He directed the research, but the day-to-day running of the group was really done by Mathew."

"Were you working with him when he-"

"Killed himself?' He closed his eyes, as though remembering. "Yes."

"Did you suspect anything was wrong?"

"I thought he had been out of sorts for a couple of weeks before it happened." He rubbed his neck.

"In what way?"

"He'd been acting secretive and stopped socialising with us."

"Did you ask him about it?"

Mike shrugged. "No. From what I knew of him, he liked to keep his private life to himself. Even when a few of us went for a drink after work, he never really opened up about himself. If he did, it was only ever in general terms- maybe about something his mum had said, or when he was going home to see his parents."

"Was he dating?" Yvonne sipped her drink, noticing that Mike had yet to touch his.

Mike hesitated.

Yvonne tried again. "Did he ever mention a girl?"

"No." Mike exhaled noisily.

"Isn't that a little unusual?"

"He was spending a *lot* of time with Carantan," Mike blurted.

"With Carantan?" Yvonne frowned. "I don't understand. Wait, are you implying he was *seeing* his professor?"

Mike wobbled his head from side-to-side. "Erm... It's what I strongly suspected at the time."

The DI took a few moments to digest this possible new connection. "Isn't that frowned upon by the university?"

"Sure. but it happens." He shrugged. "Carantan is married, too. I don't think his wife has any idea."

"Is he gay?"

Mike nodded vigorously. "Or bisexual, anyway."

"Is he out?"

"Only to a select few."

"If you thought they were having a relationship, did you wonder if it had anything to do with Mathew's death?"

Mike shrugged. "I don't know. Who can say what it is that drives people to suicide?"

Her eyes narrowed. "The coroner returned an open verdict. That sounds to me like he wasn't sure that it *was* suicide."

Mike took several slugs of his coffee, then sat with two hands around the mug, gazing into its contents. "I wouldn't know about that." He stayed, shoulders hunched. He had shrunken into himself.

Yvonne stared at his bent head, deep in thought for a few seconds, before making her excuses to leave. He had given her food for thought. Ideas swam around, needing time and space.

∽

Dewi tapped the steering wheel with his fingers, sighing every few seconds. Yvonne spotted him before he spotted her.

"Sorry. Sorry." She hurried around to the passenger side. "I just had a *very* interesting chat with one of Carantan's postgraduate students." She settled in, fastening her seat belt.

"Callum's just been in touch." Dewi's face was unusually solemn.

Yvonne screwed hers up. "Was I that long?"

"He's got a copy of the coroner's report into Mathew Hinds' death." He fired up the engine. "And, yeah. You *were* that long."

"Oh." Yvonne stared out of her window until they were out of Aberystwyth and on the road back to Newtown. "I can't wait to get stuck into that report. Do you want to hear about my conversation with Mike Jones?"

Dewi swung a brief look at her. "Sure, I'd love to. Can I nip into the next shop we come to for a sandwich?"

Yvonne put a hand up to her mouth, her eyes round in her face. "Oh Dewi, I'm sorry. Lunch. You've had no lunch." She grinned at him. "No wonder you're grumpy. My bad. Yes, let's stop and get some sandwiches to take back. You must be starving."

Dewi smiled, his eyes twinkling. "I thought you'd never notice."

An hour, two packs of sandwiches, and an interesting conversation later, and they were back in the station. Callum was waiting for them. He handed the DI a wadge of paper in a cardboard jacket. "The coroner's report, ma'am. Makes for interesting reading."

She took it to her desk and sat to peruse it fully. Callum and Dewi pulled up some chairs.

They studied the damage, marked on the diagram of Mathew's front and back. Mathew had sustained extensive bruising and broken bones in the fall. He had hemorrhaged internally, and likely died simultaneous to, or very quickly after, hitting the rocks at the bottom of the cliff. The coroner had ringed bruising to the neck and throat area and scribbled - 'unexplained by fall.'

"Hm..." Yvonne put both hands on top of her head, looking up at the ceiling as she organised her thoughts. "Was the bruising to the neck the reason for the open verdict?"

She put her eyes down again and continued working her way through. The coroner suggested that the bruising might indicate the involvement of another in Mathew's death, but he went on to say that he could not rule out Mathew having tried hanging himself, prior to jumping off the cliff.

"That sort of thing has been known before." Callum pursed his lips.

Dewi sighed. "I feel sorry for his parents. Their son, and their happiness, gone in one horrific moment and no satisfactory explanation. How do you recover from that?"

"Quite." The DI's eyes glazed over. She pictured the cliff and Mathew's last seconds. Kept seeing another figure. She could not shake the feeling there had been two people a-top that cliff. She voiced her thoughts. "But, Mathew had everything to live for. It was less than a year after he had completed his PhD thesis. He had a very important position in Carantan's research group. Why would he throw all that away?"

"Do you think his death is linked to Carantan? The affair that Mike Jones suspected?"

Yvonne rubbed her chin. "What if Mathew had threatened to expose the affair? Carantan would have been disgraced, possibly losing his position at the university and his wife into the bargain."

"True." Dewi nodded. "But, perhaps Carantan had tried to end it with Mathew, worried he could lose everything, and Mathew couldn't handle it."

"Or, Mathew discovered something in the course of the work for his thesis, maybe criminal activity, for which he paid with his life."

"This is all very well, but," Callum injected a dose of current reality to the discussion, "there is a vile group abducting children and holding them to extort money. Some of those children are from our patch. If Mathew's death is *not* linked to the abductors, we are wasting precious time."

"You're right, Callum." Yvonne bit down on the end of her pen. "I'm making links because of the ghost vehicle. We must keep in mind that this is only one line of enquiry. I hope to catch up with SOCA officers as soon as possible. Find out where they are up to. They have been awfully quiet."

18

STAKEOUT

The station was the noisiest she had heard it in a while. At one point, Yvonne put a hand over each ear. Everyone was hyped up, double-checking they had all their equipment and it was fully functional, phones and radios fully charged. Uniform and CID, alike, buzzed with purpose. The briefing room was more full than she had ever seen it. It was normally empty this time in the early evening, or else the late shift would be having their short briefing.

DCI Llewellyn entered in full uniform, chest out. There was no smile. His face muscles were unusually stiff. He had the air of someone holding their breath. He waited for the noise to die down, clearing his throat to speed up the process.

"All right, everybody."His eyes flicked around to every other pair in the room. "Today is an important day for all of us. SOCA have been working with GCHQ, and detected chatter they believe is linked with the group Vortex. They think there is a strong possibility they are going to target our area again and they believe the threat is imminent." He looked down at his papers, pursing his lips. There was silence around the room, as everyone waited for him to continue. "The Festival of Light in Dolerw Park is thought to be a strong candidate for an attempted abduction. It will be heavily attended by families from all over this part of Powys. This means we need to be on our toes. The council have switched the CCTV back on. We'll have six CID officers and as many non-uniform constables patrolling the park. You'll be our main eyes and ears. There'll be a riot van present, as a complete absence of policing would be likely to make them suspicious. The van will have its own CCTV and will be parked up outside of Oriel Gallery, to the right of the park gates. Most people will be entering through the main car park, so this van may have the clearer view." Once more, the DCI sought eye contact with every officer in the room, while Yvonne nodded encouragement.

Llewellyn continued. "Keep your eyes and your wits about you. This group is brazen and we don't know what arms they may be carrying. Don't wade in. If you see anything, call it in first and let everybody know you need back-up. Look out for each other and prioritise public safety at all times. Yvonne, you'll be coordinating your team on the ground and liaising with Inspector Griffiths regarding his uniform officers. You have the hotline to me and I have the hotline to SOCA. If anything else comes in, if I get any more intel, I will be sharing it with you if I am able. Okay, everybody, get your stuff together and get out there. Be safe."

~

A COLD RAIN WAS FALLING, whipped around by a gusty wind. It stung her face, as she left the station. She envied the uniform officers, piling into vans and cars. They could do that. Visible policing. She and her colleagues, however, would be walking the path parallel to the river, entering the park from the opposite direction. She wrapped her coat tightly around herself, turning the collar up, and adjusted her earpiece until it felt more comfortable. She turned her volume right down, until she needed it. There was always a lot of chatter, as officers sorted out last minute prep, and she found it jarring.

"Ready?" Dewi joined her, starting down the park path. Callum and Dai would be following on, several minutes behind.

Yvonne looked up at the sky. "Do you think there'll be much of a turnout in this?"

Dewi tilted his head. "Hard to say. But, if children have set their hearts on it then it'll take brave parents to tell them they can't go because of the weather."

The DI pushed her hands deep into her coat pockets, burrowing her chin into the high, woollen neck.

As they approached the main field, they could see cars already entering the car park, their occupants wisely reluctant to get out straight away. Perhaps the rain would let up, soon.

Yvonne turned a full three-hundred-and-sixty-degree circle, to get eyes on every bit of the park she could. It was quiet now, but would soon be teeming with people. "Where would they be most likely to come from, Dewi?"

"That's the problem, isn't it." Dewi frowned. "The place is so bloody open. If it was the football ground, we'd only have one entrance point to concentrate on."

Yvonne nodded. "We've got car park, the main gates, Park Street entrance, the pathway from the estates and the walkways along the river." She turned her volume up, now that the calls from other officers had died down. "I think I'll put Callum on the river paths, and Dai on the park gates. If you monitor the Park Street entrance, I'll cover the main car park and the toilet area. Debbie and Mark," she referred to two DCs, "can go amongst the main crowd."

Dewi nodded. "I'll let everyone know."

Yvonne left him to give out her instruction, whilst she headed towards the car park toilets.

The rain had stopped and the wind had quietened down. The moon broke through in patches. She checked for the mace in her right pocket, cuffs in her left, as though some dark force might have extracted them without her knowledge. She relaxed at their feel. She had chosen sturdy flat shoes, though she was wearing a skirt beneath her long coat. The earlier, biting rain had her regretting that wardrobe choice. She had felt it would make her less obvious.

She took a seat on the long, low wall that divided the town centre from the park. To her front right was the toilet block, and beyond that the main car park. Directly ahead of her, a large grass area with pavement. Behind her, the town lights and the busy road leading to back lane.

People approached from every direction and there were a lot of families. Small children, clutching fluorescent tubes or else, holding up rotating kaleidoscope fans, their colour patterns constantly changing. She had to be careful not to stare too long for fear of seeing those patterns in front of her eyes. She thought of her nephew and niece, Tom and Sally. They would have loved this. She was glad they were not here.

"Everything okay?" She spoke into the microphone, inside the high collar of her coat. Several replies came back from around the field. All quiet. Nothing out of the ordinary. If she was a smoker, she would have lit up. She felt out of place, sitting alone on the wall. She made the crowd-searching obvious, as though she were waiting for someone.

From Back Lane direction, to her right, a procession of giant lanterns approached. Each was the shape of an animal. There were fish, birds and larger mammals. Each lantern was carried by two people and the long line made for an impressive sight. A cheer went up from the crowd and she could hear the excitement of the children. She looked back at the main crowd. To date, only teenagers had been taken and it was these she monitored most. The smallest children tended to be holding their guardians' hands, or else were on their father's shoulders. No, it was the young teenagers who Vortex appeared to be targeting. They would be most likely to be on the fringes of the crowd, shunning their parents' hands. Or just shunning their parents.

"Do you mind if I sit here?"

The question made her jump.

A woman in her thirties had sat on the wall next to her, searching her bag for something. A look of relief flooded her face as she removed her mobile phone and punched a number into it.

Yvonne was unsure whether she minded. On the one hand, the close presence of another was comforting. On the other, she had a job to do and the woman was partially obscuring her view. The lady, herself, was clearly not worried either way.

The smell of burger and onions wafted across the field and a band was playing somewhere on the field. She stood up. The crowd was now at such levels she would need to start walking around to properly monitor it.

Lots of people were in dark clothing and had their hoods up. If potential abductors were amongst the crowds, they were going to be much harder to spot. Once or twice, she followed young men she felt looked suspicious but nothing came of it. Over an hour passed like this, before the rain came again.

A huge whale lantern, with a thick wooden frame, had been purposely set alight. It lit up the field and warmed the crowd's faces. It created loud whooshing noises, whenever a gust of wind blew through. The DI's feet ached and her eyes hurt from the smoke and the searching. She needed a hot drink and her bed.

The burning of the whale over, the crowd began to disperse. This was another danger period. Yvonne refocussed, walking faster amongst the disappearing crowd. Nothing. The radio was silent.

∼

BEDRAGGLED officers filed in for the nine o'clock debrief, their faces said it all. Shoulders hunched, saying little, they removed bits of kit, throwing them into the their lockers and handing in dying batteries.

Yvonne knew how they felt. There wasn't a single officer there who would have wanted a child to be under threat. But, equally, they had all wanted to catch someone in the attempt. Make some headway with the case. Tired, wet and hungry, she overheard one uniformed officer say it had been a, "crap-shoot," and that, "SOCA needed to get their facts straight."

Whereas the room had been hyper only hours before, it was now a morgue, as Llewellyn thanked them all for their participation. "At least we can say that no-one was abducted and that may have been down to your vigilance."

"I don't think they tried for this event, sir." Dai Clayton rose from his chair to leave.

Llewellyn nodded. "You may be right. Either way, you did a good job out there and people were reassured by the visible presence by uniform."

Yvonne walked up to the DCI. "It can't be helped, sir, I know. I think everyone thought we might get a result. They'll be fine in the morning."

Llewellyn nodded. "Before you go, Yvonne, SOCA have asked that we stake out the Newtown Winter fair, next week."

"The fifteenth?"

"Yes. It's the other event where they thought an abduction attempt would likely take place. Is that a problem?"

Yvonne thought about it. The fifteenth was her birthday. Her fortieth birthday. The big four-o. She had been looking forward to doing something with Kim and the children. Her eyes soulful, she thought of the youngsters held captive. Thought of their sadness, loneliness and fear. She thought of their parents and the utter terror they must be feeling. She raised those soulful eyes to the DCI's. "No, Chris. It's not a problem. I'll prep the team. We'll be ready."

19

FRUSTRATION

Donna placed her cool hand on Kyle's forehead. He was hot to the touch. Though sleeping, his rest was fitful, and every now and then he gave a weak cough. She poured a little of their precious water onto the young boy's hair and wet his lips.

Peter paced the floor, muttering angrily to himself.

Donna left Kyle's side to grab Peter's arm. "Pete, come and sit down. You're going to wear yourself out. You'll fall ill, too, and I don't know how I'd cope with two of you to look after."

He moved as though he was going to brush her hand off him, but thought better of it. He stared down into her face. "What time do you reckon it is?"

She shrugged. "I dunno, afternoon sometime, maybe two o'clock?"

He left her to go and kick the door with a loud bang. "Are you going to let us have some food in here?" He put his ear to the door, pulling back to kick the door again. "Hey! There's a sick child in here. He needs medical attention." Peter turned back to Donna. "I haven't heard anyone today.

Not a sound. Do you think they've abandoned us? Left us here and just gone?"

Donna shook her head. "I don't know." She felt real fear at that thought. She joined Peter at the door and they both listened. Still nothing.

Peter pulled away. "Stand back from the door, Donna."

"What are you going to do?" Her voice shook.

"This." Peter backed several paces before launching himself at the door.

Donna recoiled from the sickening thud, as the door failed to give way. Peter doubled over, nursing his shoulder.

Donna shot a look over to Kyle. He was still sleeping. She went to Peter, placing her hand on his back. "Come on. Come and sit with us. I'm sure they'll bring food soon."

There were tears in Peter's eyes as he stood. Donna's heart went out to him. She placed an arm around his waist. He returned with her to sit on the bed.

20

SLIPPERY

"Dr. Carantan?" Yvonne ran up the steps to the Computer Sciences department, as he walking through the main entrance. She was late. The journey from Newtown had been a fraught affair. She had spent nearly thirty minutes of it stuck behind a horse-box and she had already been late leaving the station. Half of the trip, she spent swearing under her breath.

Carantan took his time turning around. "Inspector Giles." He placed his hands in his trouser pockets.

"Thank you for agreeing to see me, again." She stopped to catch her breath and steady herself.

"Well, if I didn't know better, I'd be wondering if you'd developed a crush on me."

She wasn't sure if he was grinning or sneering at her. His movements were unhurried, shoulders relaxed. The DI felt self-conscious. She attempted a smile but managed only a small movement with her mouth. She felt off-kilter, still tired from the night before and the uneventful stake-out of the festival.

"Come on in." He held the door open for her. She

noticed that the sleeves of his thin, black pullover were rolled up to his elbows. His forearms were lean but muscular. The way he looked at her, as she passed him, made the hairs rise on the back of her neck. She wished she had brought Dewi or another member of her team.

She followed him down a well-lit corridor, to a door with his name on it. He opened it and motioned her in.

To her left was a desk covered in piles of books and random pieces of paper. On the wall behind it, a medium-sized white board, covered in flow charts. Against the wall to her right, ran a row of armless soft chairs. He indicated for her to take a seat on them.

She took out her notebook.

Carantan sat behind his desk.

"So, what can I help you with?" He looked down at her notebook and then back into her face, his own face expressionless.

"I wanted to talk to you about Mathew Hinds."

His head jerked back, his eyes boring into her.

She continued. "I understand he worked for you as post-doc."

He placed his hands together, as though in prayer, elbows on his desk and his lips resting on his fingertips. He stayed like that for a couple of seconds.

Yvonne cleared her throat.

"Yes. Mathew Hinds was my research assistant." He looked away to the window. "Why do you want to talk to me about Mathew?"

She sat back in her chair. "I believe there may be a connection to a major case we are working on. I think someone who knew Mathew is involved in criminal activity. I came to you to learn more about him and his work in computer science."

"Ah, yes. You said that a vehicle had been registered to one of my empty flats and in Mathew's name."

"That's right."

He sighed. "What would you like to know? Mathew was hard-working, intelligent and with a very interesting mind. He had a knack for the unusual. He was hugely creative in his problem-solving. In a different life, he could have been an artist."

"What was he working on before he died?"

Carantan ran a hand through his hair. The mussed look and his wild eyebrows gave him a fierce air. His voice was soft. "It was a continuation of his post-graduate work, really. He was examining the potential of cryptocurrency, weighing up its pros and cons. He believed in it being a force for good but was exploring the pitfalls. His father lost a lot of money during the financial crash, when Mathew was in his teens. Many banks were refusing to lend to businesses, including his father's. Cryptocurrency was created as a viable alternative to the high-street banks. It's policed by peer-to-peer checking, across the global network. Highly accurate, as every computer has a list of every transaction and so can verify whether a transaction can go ahead or not. Once a transaction is agreed, it becomes part of the record owned by all computers in the system. This is an unchangeable record, known as a blockchain. Matthew was fascinated by the idea, but was looking at the downsides, for example, the possibilities of fraudulent information being coded into the blockchains."

The DI shook her head. "You've lost me, I'm afraid."

"You probably don't need to worry about the details, Inspector, just that Mathew's and my research was looking deep into the programming and algorithms used in the mining of cryptocurrencies and in its use in the dark web which, at that time, was in its infancy."

"The dark web." More ideas swam around her brain, as she tried to make sense of what she was hearing. Her eyes returned to Carantan. "How did you get on, on a personal level?" She kept her expression and her body language open.

He stared at her, she could almost sense his brain weighing up how much he could safely say.

She decided a prompt might help. "Were you friends outside of work?"

He frowned. "What do you mean, Inspector?"

"Were you close?"

He stared at her in silence.

"I'm sorry." She sighed. "I'll be blunt. I've been informed that you may have been having a relationship and I wanted to ask you if this was true?"

He shook his head. "Where did you hear that? And, what has that to do with the case you are supposed to be investigating?"

"As we've already discussed, his details were used to register a vehicle we are looking for and, as we delved into his background, we discovered that the coroner had returned an open verdict on his death."

"What is your point?"

"My point is that no-one can be sure exactly how he died. It is not the established suicide that many people were led to believe. The coroner couldn't rule out the involvement of another in Mathew's death."

"Oh, I get it." His contorted face betrayed his disgust. "You hear from some seedy source that I had been having a romantic relationship with Mathew and you begin to suspect that I had a hand in his death. Is that it? Is that what you think? What, you think *I* threw him off that cliff?"

"Dr. Carantan, I-"

"Get out. Get out. And, the next time you wish to come here accusing me of murder, bring a warrant!" His face, still contorted, was now bright red, his fists clenched.

Yvonne stood up, brushing down her skirt. "Thank you for your time," she said, as calmly as she could manage. "I'll see myself out."

After she had left the building, she leaned with her back to it and took several deep breaths. Carantan clearly had a temper and she had just been on the wrong side of it. Her legs only just managed to get her to the car.

She was still feeling out of sorts as she arrived at Gannets restaurant, in the back streets behind Aberystwyth Castle, where she was due to meet Tasha for lunch.

21

RESPITE

Tasha was already seated at the table, in the tiny restaurant with a big reputation. Yvonne had never eaten there. It was Tasha's discovery and she had given it high praise indeed. The DI was hoping her appetite would return in time for the food.

"Are you all right?" Tasha tilted her head, concerned, as she stood to greet her friend.

Yvonne managed a weak smile. "I will be," she said, as she pulled out a chair and sat.

"Difficult day?"

"Difficult interview."

Yvonne glanced around. Aside from the sign outside and the large, glass window at the front, they could have been in someone's house. They were seated at a round table in the corner and only two other tables were occupied. The smell coming from the kitchen made both their mouths water. Yvonne need not have worried about her appetite. The decor was homely, and black-and-white autographed stills of celebrity diners were dotted around the walls.

Yvonne felt the tension easing from her.

"Glass of wine?" Tasha enquired, holding up a half-carafe.

The DI put her hand up. "I'm driving *and* I'm on duty."

Tasha grinned. "I thought that would be your answer. Hence, the half-carafe of table wine. I caught the bus. It travels along the prom. Great views."

The DI eyed Tasha's glass with envy. "Shame, I could have done with one of those."

"It's very good. Mm, Mmmm." Tasha gave her a teasing grin.

Yvonne gave her a gentle slap on the arm. "Stop it."

"Why don't you call in sick, this afternoon. Stay over?"

Yvonne shook her head. "I can't. We've got way too much on for me to take a whole afternoon. What have you ordered?"

"Sea bass. But, I can recommend the sirloin. All of the food here is excellent."

The bespectacled manageress came to take their orders. Yvonne decided on the sirloin and the waitress left to take the order to the chef and to get Yvonne an orange juice.

"So, come on. Who was the difficult interview?"

Yvonne kicked her shoes off and leaned her head back against the top of her high-backed chair. She proceeded to tell Tasha about the case and the potential tie-in with Mathew Hinds, finishing with her difficult interview with Carantan.

"This isn't for public consumption," she reminded Tasha.

"No, of course not." The psychologist took another sip of wine. "Are you wondering if he reacted out of guilt?"

"Maybe. What do you think?"

Tasha thought about it for a moment. "Difficult to say without being present but, if he had genuine feelings for

Mathew, his reaction could have come from a place of hurt."

Yvonne pursed her lips. "He's married. Something about him makes me very uncomfortable. I just can't put my finger on what."

"I wish I'd been there," Tasha said, just as their food arrived.

For the next minute or so, they were lulled by the gentle background music and soft chatter from the other guests as they tucked into food which had been cooked to perfection.

"You have good taste." Yvonne wiped her mouth on her napkin. "This is really good."

Tasha laughed. "What? You've taken this long to realise that?" Her eyes sparkled. "So, what's your next move going to be? And, isn't your fortieth birthday coming up soon?"

Yvonne sighed. "Oh yes, I'd forgotten."

"We should do something." Tasha rubbed her cheek. "What do you fancy?"

Yvonne shook her head, the corners of her mouth turning down. "You're not going to believe this, but I'm going to be working on my birthday."

"Actually, I *can* believe it, but I am disappointed. Is there no way you can have a little time off?"

'Not really, Tasha." Yvonne sighed. "My birthday coincides with the Newtown winter fair. It's going to be a big one and SOCA, in their wisdom, have pointed to it as a strong candidate for a potential abduction by Vortex. We need all hands on deck to stake it out. That is the evening gone, and most of the day will be spent planning it."

"You don't sound to sure about SOCA." Tasha searched the DI's face.

"Well, it's just that we staked out a festival last night in the wind and rain on their intelligence and nothing came of it. Not that I wanted an abduction to happen," she added. "It's just, we so badly hoped we'd catch someone in the attempt."

Tasha put down her knife and fork and picked up her glass. "I'm sure they, like other intelligence agencies, are working with probabilities. They almost never get the complete picture, just bits and pieces that they have to string together to second guess what might happen. Are they talking to you?"

Yvonne shook her head. "Not to me. They are liaising with the DCI, though, and he is unusually tight-lipped about the whole thing."

"I saw some of the viral posts on social media. Are people paying the ransom?"

"According to SOCA, yes. It's hard to stop people when you're dealing with the dark web. And, these are children. It's getting every decent person in the gut. Our instincts are to help. No decent person wants to see children suffer. In theory, people could be prosecuted for paying. But, I don't think that will happen. I certainly hope not, anyway."

Tasha nodded agreement. "You can't punish people for caring."

"I just hope it doesn't encourage them to take more youngsters. It doesn't bear thinking about."

Yvonne finished her plate of food and Tasha downed the rest of her wine.

"Feeling okay?" Yvonne nodded towards Tasha's empty glass.

Tasha grinned and the DI could see from her eyes that she was, perhaps a little tipsy.

"Come on, you. I'll order you a coffee to take out and I'll give you a lift to the bus stop."

"Take the afternoon off." Tasha gave her a wicked smile.

"I'm tempted." Yvonne laughed. "But, I'm not going to. I tell you what. When this case is all over, we'll do this again. Maybe choose a restaurant closer to your home in Aberdovey and I'll stay. How's that?"

"Perfect."

∼

Yvonne pushed her front door closed with her foot, car keys between her teeth and hands full of shopping bags and handbag. She placed the bags in the hallway with a sigh of relief, examining the painful indents where the handles had dug in. She put the keys onto the hook on the wall and her coat on a peg, before taking a deep breath and raising the shopping once more, to take it through to the kitchen. The final leg.

She found the chardonnay in the fridge. After pouring herself a generous glass, she stood for several minutes, eyes red-rimmed and glazed over, pondering the week's events. She rubbed her sore hands. The redness in the indents had faded.

She thought of Mathew Hinds. Had he tried to hang himself and then changed his mind, before going to the cliff-top, like someone who makes a few practice marks with the knife, before finally slashing their wrists? Or had someone accompanied him up that cliff? Someone he trusted? Perhaps, someone he loved? What had he felt in those last few moments? Fear or desperation?

She took a long, cool sip of the chardonnay, leaning back against the countertop, and closed her eyes.

The shrill sound of the telephone jerked her painfully into the here and now. She placed down her glass with a sigh and, kicking off her shoes, ran to the phone in her stockinged feet.

"Hello?"

"Yvonne? It's Kim."

Her heart leapt at hearing her sister's voice. She had missed her. "Kim. How are you? How are the children?"

"We're great here, Yvonne. Busy as ever. Children enjoying school and making a mess for me. I've just settled them down to sleep. It took five stories tonight. Five stories. Little monkeys."

Yvonne laughed. "I can't wait to read them a bedtime story again, Kim. You don't know how lucky you are."

Kim chuckled. "You're right. I wouldn't change a thing. But, talking about you reading them a bedtime story, I wanted to talk to you about your birthday."

"Oh, yes. The big one."

"Yeah. The kids and I are coming down on the day. We will be with you in the afternoon, if you're not working, or when you get home, if you are."

Yvonne sighed. "Kim-"

"We'll have food out and when we've tucked the kids up, we'll get out the wine... or the gin."

"Kim."

"What? What's up? Are you doing something else?" Kim's tone had lowered and Yvonne could picture the confused sadness, creeping over her sister's face.

"No, I'm not doing anything else. At least, not anything I will enjoy. I would love nothing more than to see you and the children. I've missed you all so much. I can't wait to cuddle the little ones again. But, I have to work and I have to work in the evening. It's a major case and a major operation. It'll be taking place throughout the evening. I'm really sorry."

"Will you have to travel on your birthday?" Kim sounded concerned.

"No. No, I won't have to travel. It's a surveillance op at an event in Newtown. It won't be over until late. Please don't repeat that to anyone."

"Of course not," Kim reassured.

"I so wish it could have been on another day."

"Bad timing, eh?"

"Yeah. Can we do it another time? Maybe the following weekend? Depending on how you are fixed?"

"Yeah, sure." Kim sighed. "Well, have a great one. I will phone you in the week. Give me a ring on the big day if you get a chance sometime during your big op. We'd really like to say happy birthday."

Yvonne smiled into the phone. "I will, Kim. I promise. Give my love and very big hugs to the children and tell them I *will* see them soon."

22

SOCA

Lucas and Lyons were back. They had been in conference with Llewellyn for most of the morning. When they surfaced, they asked to speak with the rest of the team, on a casual basis. They appeared to be going around each member, in turn.

Yvonne kept one eye on them, while helping Dewi make the coffees.

"What do they mean, a casual basis? Who says that?"

Dewi laughed. "Well, I guess we'll find out. But, if I were a betting man, I'd bet they're just wanting to make sure we're not blabbing our mouths off to anyone about the operation."

Yvonne thought about Tasha and began pulling at her lip. "Why would we do that? In any case, they haven't exactly told us anything of what they are up to. What's to blab about?"

George Lucas approached from behind. "Ooh. Are we just in time for the coffees?"

Yvonne swung round, faint colour rising on her cheeks. "Of course, how do you like them?" She turned back to the drinks, wondering if Lucas had heard any of their conversation.

"Black, one sugar, thank you. Mark likes his white with two."

"Right." Yvonne pulled a couple more mugs out of the cupboard, looking inside to check they were clean.

"You're the DI, aren't you? Yvonne, wasn't it?" Lucas' friendly air seemed genuine enough.

She turned around to speak with him. Dewi took over the coffee-making.

"That's right." She held out her hand. "Yvonne Giles. I hear you've been busy working alongside GCHQ."

He nodded, taking his hands out of his pockets to shake hers. "Kind of. We're not so much working alongside them. It's more them doing us a few favours. They've been helping isolate possible communications between the group."

"Wow. That's a big deal, isn't it?"

"It's difficult." He sighed. "The problem we're having is that they're using their own code, and communications appear to come in tiny, controlled bursts. After a couple of to-and-fros, they're back to radio silence. Maybe, for days. We believe they remove the sims from their devices and are changing sims frequently. Pay-as-you-go. They're keeping net chat, even on the dark web, to a minimum."

Yvonne frowned. "Aside from their sick go-fund-me take-offs."

"Right."

"But, surely, GCHQ will have narrowed down where these guys are by now, won't they? Even from so few communications. I mean, if they know the messages *are* between members of Vortex?"

"They're not texting from their base. They're moving to other locations to send their messages. The sims go live in a particular location for a few minutes, at most. Then, they go dark again."

"Oh."

"Yeah."

"How do they know the messages are from the group?"

"They crack, or partially crack, their code each time-"

"Wait, Vortex change their code for each bunch of communications?"

"Looks that way. They obviously work to a system. We haven't cracked that, yet."

"Do you think they are using complex computer systems for generating the codes? Some sort of algorithm, maybe?"

He jerked his head back. "Wow. That's a bit deep for me, maybe I should take you to GCHQ." His laugh was deep and gutteral.

Yvonne joined in. "Hardly, I don't really know much of what I'm talking about. Sounded good though, didn't it?" She grinned, shrugging. "I was looking through a computer scientist's post-graduate thesis the other day. Picked up a few buzz words."

"The DCI tells me you've been hunting down leads, around the vehicle used to abduct one of the victims."

"That's right." Yvonne nodded, her gaze pensive. "The vehicle was registered to a dead research assistant and an empty flat. That post-graduate thesis I mentioned? It was his."

"Really?"

"Really. And, what's more, he'd been researching the possibilities regarding fraudulent coding into the blockchains used in cryptocurrency management."

Lucas pulled a face. "There you go again."

"Yeah. Sorry." She pursed her lips. "Anyway, the young man in question died just over three years ago. At the time, it was hyped up to be a suicide. In actual fact, the coroner had returned an open verdict, and it was clear from his report that he had suspicions of foul play. Though, unfortunately, nothing that could be proved either way."

"I see." Lucas stared at the floor, rubbing his chin.

Dewi pushed his coffee towards him, just as Mark Lyons joined them. Yvonne noted that Lyons was dressed more casually. Jeans and jumper. Lucas was in another suit, tie loosened.

"You've given me food for thought, DI Giles, even though you did mash my brain with science." Lucas winked at her.

She could have felt patronised at this, but gave him the benefit of the doubt. "Anytime." She gave him a mock courtesy.

∼

STUCK IN TRAFFIC, on her way home from what had felt like a very long day, Yvonne turned the radio on. The six o'clock news was just starting and, not for the first time, it was dominated by the exploits of Vortex. She turned the volume up.

'In their latest video release, Vortex have threatened to carry out more abductions, if the payments to them are not increased in line with their demands. They are also threatening to torture and kill the youngsters they are holding. The prime minister has issued a statement, saying that Britain will not surrender to cyberterrorism and will not pay ransom to the kidnappers. A cobra meeting has been called to discuss the latest threats and demands.'

She turned the radio off. What the newscasters had not been able to report was the sheer number of agencies now involved in hunting down the extortionist group. They knew how the group were communicating with each other and how orders were being relayed. They were now in a desperate race to locate where they were holding the hostages, when they could deploy special forces and crack police teams.

She thought about her team and the relatively small part they were playing in the overall picture. If they could identify even one member of the snatch group, they could potentially help blow open the whole case. Perhaps, on her birthday. Perhaps, at the fair.

23

TRAGEDY

Newtown station was alive with noisy activity once again, as officers rushed to and fro, gathering and checking equipment and vehicles. Double-checking they knew where they were going to be and who they needed to report to.

Yvonne spread the park and town centre map on the table in the briefing room.

"As last time, we'll be looking to have our eyes on the entrances and exits to the park. We can't arrive too early. We wait until the first crowds begin to arrive, before moving into position. Callum, you're on the river paths. Dewi, you have Park Street entrance. Debbie and Mark, you'll be wandering amongst the crowds, where you'll be fully supported by plain clothes PCs. Dai, you'll be on the park gates. Everyone okay with their roll and where they are supposed to be?"

"All good." Dewi nodded, and he was joined in his affirmation by the other members of the group.

"Great. I'm going to be around the main car park, the bridge over the river and the toilet area. If we see anything suspicious, anything at all, we call it in. If you see an attempted abduction you call on everyone to go, go, go. I don't need to tell you that this event will bring its own challenges. The festival of light was a fairly quiet affair. Tonight we'll have loud music, fair rides and people shouting over microphones. It'll be a struggle to hear each other, so try to keep one eye on your colleagues, whenever possible. Don't worry about vehicles, concentrate on the people. Uniform will be looking for suspicious vehicles and monitoring them. If a snatch gang does come to our fair, we have to get them all. From what we can tell, the gangs communicate by mobile phone, in controlled, short bursts and take the sims out of their phones at all other times. Vortex won't be expecting an immediate confirmation of a snatch. That buys SOCA time to interrogate the abductors. That can only work if we have them all. So, if you think you have eyes on, unless it's an active snatch, you covertly alert everyone else, so that we can observe and locate all operators, before the take down. Is everybody clear?"

Again, there were nods all round. The DI took a deep breath. "Check your equipment is fully functional before going out. Be vigilant. Be safe."

∾

YVONNE SCANNED THE CROWDS. She estimated there were at least a couple of thousand people present and the mood was good. Whenever she saw children wandering away from their parents, she watched on tenterhooks, until the parents reeled them in. At this rate, by the end of the night, her nerves would be shot.

As she walked around her patch of the park, she achieved occasional visuals on each member of her team. They were working hard. She scanned around the exits.

There were plenty of youngsters wearing hooded tops, she monitored all the ones she could see, for a couple of seconds each. Nothing jumped out at her. Just kids enjoying themselves.

A gloved hand covered each of her eyes.

"Surprise!"

She almost jumped into the air, spinning round to remonstrate with the person behind her, realising as she did, that it was her sister, Kim.

"Bloody hell, Kim! What are you doing here?"

Her sister leaned in, to shout into her ear. "I came to see you. Happy Birthday. I'll leave you to your work and we'll catch up with you later."

Yvonne felt guilty and gave her sister a hug. "Where's Tom and Sally? You left them with someone?"

"They're here." Kim looked to the sides and then behind her, a look of confusion coming over her face. "They were right here." Kim took a few paces towards a food van, to see if her children had headed that way.

Yvonne's heart thudded in her chest as she joined her sister in looking for them. Moving in and around the throngs of people, their searching became more frantic.

"What are they wearing?" Yvonne shouted to her sister.

Kim frowned in concentration. "Er... Sally's wearing a pink dress and a grey duffle coat. Tom is in brown trousers and a... a cream jumper."

Yvonne took her sister's arm, calling into her ear. "Kim, listen. Keep looking. I'm going to put a call out to all of my colleagues to keep an eye out for them. Go to the man holding the mike, by the waltzers, and get him to ask for them to go to him."

Kim stood frozen, her face contorted with panic.

"Go. Go." Yvonne ordered and her sister snapped out of

it. The DI was trembling, afraid the children may have been taken by Vortex. She gave herself a mental shake. Even if the gang had turned up in this field, the chances that they would have chosen her nephew and niece were slim, given the size of the crowd. That thought gave her comfort, but there was still no sign of the little ones. She ducked behind the toilet block and put a call out to all police in the park.

"Keep your eyes open for two small children, most likely together. A boy, answering to the name of Tom, aged six years with dark brown hair and wearing a cream jumper and brown trousers. And his sister, Sally, aged seven and with blonde, wavy hair. She's wearing a pink dress and grey duffle coat. If you see them, please detain them and let me know, immediately."

The music quietened down and a call came over the loudspeakers, from the man operating the waltzers. "Could Tom and Sally, that's Tom and Sally, please come here to the waltzers, your mommy is waiting for you. That's Tom and Sally, Tom and Sally, please come to your mommy at the waltzers."

The music came back up. Yvonne went from stall to stall, looking in every direction, scanning every small child she could. But, there was no sign of her nephew and niece. Her mobile vibrated in her pocket.

She fumbled for it, pulling it out and almost dropping it in the process. It was Dewi. "Dewi? Have you found them?"

"No. No, I'm sorry I haven't. I was ringing to ask you if you'd found them. What's going on?"

Yvonne wanted to cry. "Dewi, they're my nephew and niece. My sister brought them here, wanting to surprise me on my birthday. She knew I was working but she didn't know what I was working on or she would never have brought the children here."

"I'm coming over to you." Dewi's voice was firm. "I'll get a plain clothes PC to cover my patch."

She knew she ought to order him not to. This op was too important and yet, she could not bring herself to do it. She needed the children found and her head was scrambled by terror. She no longer trusted herself. She spotted him running through the crowd towards her, face determined.

He grabbed both her upper arms. "It's going to be okay. Any minute now they'll show up with their mum. Look at me." He searched her face. "Little kids wander off. I lost count of the number of times mine did when they were this age. We *will* find them."

KIM CAME RUNNING TO HER, crying and shaking, her red woollen hat lopsided, scarf falling loose. "Where are they? Where are they?"

Yvonne placed her arms around her. "They'll show up. We've got people searching for them all over the park. The control room have also put out an area-wide alert. We'll find them, sis. We'll find them."

As she said this, a couple of female officers approached Kim with a blanket and a plastic cup of tea. One of them had her notebook open, ready to take a statement. From where she stood, the DI could see a couple of male officers alighting from a dog van, closely followed by two large alsatians.

Yvonne ran up to Kim. "Do you have anything of children's on you? Anything at all?"

Kim reached into her bag and pulled out a small rag doll. "This is Sally's." She held the doll out and Yvonne grabbed it. Heading off in the direction of the dog team.

Sirens could be heard, intermittently, from the direction

of the car park. Many more uniformed officers had been drafted in and were stopping people and talking to them, as they began leaving the park.

She passed the doll to dog handlers, explaining it was Sally's, then headed back to find Dewi.

"Make sure we get every bit off CCTV footage," she shouted to him. The children disappeared from somewhere near that food van."

"On it, ma'am." Dewi wandered off.

Left alone, Yvonne bent double, struggling to get her breath. The ground swam and wobbled beneath her. She held her sides, fighting to stay upright. She became aware of the alsatians, who had caught a scent, near the food van. She tried to focus on them, but collapsed.

When she came round, she was on her back on the ground. Two members of the St. John's Ambulance were administering to her, the light bouncing off their high-vis jacket strips. Her mouth and nose were covered by a plastic mask. One of the medics squeezed air into it with regular rhythm. Slowly, everything came back into focus.

"Yvonne. Yvonne, can you hear me?"

Her eyes met those of the medic calling to her. She nodded.

"Has this happened before?"

She nodded again.

"We're going to lift you onto a stretcher and get you checked over at the hospital, okay?"

She shook her head, struggling to get up. "No." Her voice was garbled through the mask. She pulled it off. "Not the hospital. It's just a panic attack. I get them." She made to rise and her head swam again. "I don't need the hospital."

Kim's face appeared over her. "Go to the hospital, sis.

Your colleagues are looking after me. Get yourself checked out, please. I'm so sorry about all this."

Yvonne did not want her sister to feel sorry. As she was stretchered into the ambulance, she promised her she would be back within half an hour.

24

CCTV NIGHTMARE

In reality, it was several hours before she was released, and then only under duress. The hospital had wanted to keep her in overnight for observation. She signed herself out at two am, getting the only taxi available, from Shrewsbury back to Newtown, at the cost of sixty pounds.

She joined members of her team and her sister back at the station following a fruitless search for the children.

"We've gathered all the CCTV from around the town and park and we're going through it now." Dewi put a hand on her shoulder. "The DCI is here. Why don't you take your sister home and get some rest. You can trust us. If the children are on the CCTV footage, we'll find out what happened and do what we have to do to begin getting them back. We don't need you here to be able to do that, ma'am, and you can come at it again tomorrow, when you're fresh."

As though in support of what her DS was saying, her traitorous body gave over to yawning, her knees shaking and threatening to give way. She felt physically and emotionally exhausted.

"All right, Dewi. I'll take Kim home. But, if anything

changes or you have any news, please, please call me. I love those children like they are my own and my sister is in pieces. Keep us informed."

Dewi nodded. "I will, ma'am. I promise."

∿

AT EIGHT-THIRTY, the following morning, Newtown station was eerily quiet. Yvonne had left Kim with liaison officers who were supporting her and making sure they had full details of what had taken place the night before.

Dai Clayton sat alone, playing and replaying CCTV footage. He started, when he heard her footfall behind him. When he turned to her, he looked pale, his eyes rimmed with red.

"Have you been here all night?" She pulled out a chair to sit next to him.

"No, ma'am. I haven't been here long. I didn't get home until three am, though, so I haven't had much sleep. The others were still here when I left, so I guess they won't be back just yet."

"Is anyone at the crime scene?" She rubbed her head in a vain attempt to ward off a developing headache.

"SOCO are working it, ma'am. It's cordoned off to the public though..." He grimaced. "It's obviously already somewhat contaminated."

"And the dogs? Did they pick up a scent?"

"They did. They followed the scent to The Mound." He was referring to the remains of the Norman motte and bailey fort. "The scent ended there, I'm afraid."

"So, they were most likely extracted from there by vehicle."

"Seems likely." He pointed to his computer screen and

the fuzzy image of two men wearing dark clothing and hoodies. "They found these suspects in two pieces of footage. I must warn you that one of the excerpts has children in it. We believe them to be Tom and Sally, but we need you or their mother to confirm that for us." His eyes searched her face. "Are you sure you are okay with this?"

"Are you kidding me? I have to see them, Dai. Wait, were they harmed?"

"No, not that we can tell. In fact, in this footage, they don't seem distressed, so they may not have realised what was happening to them."

"No, they probably wouldn't have. They're very young. And if the men acted friendly..." She sighed, shaking her head. "They're so trusting."

Dai gave her forearm a squeeze, before he tapped 'play' on the first piece of footage.

The clip was about fifteen seconds long and showed the area next to the food van, timed eight-fifteen pm.

Two dark figures with their hoods up approached two children from behind.

"That's them. That's Tom and Sally." Yvonne hands shot up to her face.

One of the figures tapped Tom on the shoulder to talk to him. In the background, Yvonne's sister Kim had put her hands over Yvonne's eyes.

"Oh my god. That's when they did it. She had her back turned for seconds." Yvonne shook her head.

The figures had picked up the children, giving them shoulder rides. They disappeared behind the food van. The clip ended.

"As fast as that. It took moments."

"That's right." Dai readied the other video clip.

"We've got to get them back. Please god, we must get

them back." Tears streamed down her face.

"Are you ready for the next?"

She nodded. "Yes."

A white van was shown moving along New Road, in the Welshpool direction. Dai zoomed in on the plate and back out again. "They ran the plate last night. It's registered to a Ford Fiesta in Telford." Dai sighed. "They didn't ghost this one. They duplicated a plate."

"How many CCTVs did it pass? Surely, we can locate where it ended up?"

Dai shook his head. "None of the main cameras picked the van up again. I ran another check when I got in this morning but nothing's been logged. West Mercia have been looking for anything they've got and nothing. I think the kidnappers parked up, somewhere away from the cameras, and switched plates."

Yvonne sat, a haunted look in her sunken eyes. "I let this happen. I took my eye off the ball. They were in my area of the park."

"Hey, come on. You weren't to know your sister would surprise you. Don't beat yourself up." Dai rose from his seat to put an arm around her shoulders. "The others will be back any minute. Come on, I'll make you a brew."

∾

CAMERA FLASHLIGHTS LIT up in volleys, all across the front of the stage. The click, click, click and the constant barrage of questions as they filed onto the stage, brought on waves of nausea. Yvonne followed DCI Llewelyn, followed by her sister, Kim. They each sat behind a microphone. Kim, dishevelled and tearful, drank several mouthfuls of water. Yvonne fingered her pen with a trembling hand.

The DCI kicked off the press conference. "Thank you all for attending today. I'm DCI Llewelyn and next to me is DI Giles. As you will all know, two of our young children were abducted last night from Dolerw Park, in Newtown. In a few moments, their mother, Ms Kimberley Knowles, will address you all and make her public appeal. I can tell you that we have not heard from whoever took the children. They have not, as yet, made any attempt to contact us. We have CCTV footage of the perpetrators and will be making it public later today. We also need your help in tracing a white transit van that we believe was involved in the abduction. The number for the enquiry line is the one you see in front of this desk. The public can also supply information on our 101 line. Please contact us with any information you have, no matter how small you think it might be. Your information could prove pivotal. I will now hand you over to the children's mum, Kimberley."

Yvonne gave Kim a reassuring smile and squeezed her hand.

Kim swallowed hard. Brushing her fringe away from her eyes, she took another sip of water. The room was the quietest Yvonne had heard it.

Kim cleared her throat. "I'd like to talk first of all to my babies, Tom and Sally. If you can hear me, your mummy loves you so very much and I am doing everything I can to bring you back home to me. Please look after each other." Tears dropped onto the table and Kim surpassed a sob with her hand. She opened up a crumpled note paper and began reading. "To the people who took my children, I'd just like to say that I'm not judging you and I'm not looking to get you punished, I just want my babies back. They are my whole world and they are so young. Remember that little things can frighten ones so young and so innocent. Please,

please treat them with kindness and care. Please don't scare them. Please don't hurt them." Kim's voice shook with emotion and her chest heaved. "They are the kindest, funniest, most gentle children in the world. Please, bring them home. Please let them go. They are so loved."

Yvonne put her hand over her sister's and kept it there. Her sister had been so strong and dignified in her address. Her pain was palpable.

The room was quiet for several seconds before the barrage of lights and questions began again. The DCI thanked everyone for taking the time to attend and signalled for Yvonne and Kim to rise. As they began filing out again, Llewellyn asked to see Yvonne in his office. She reluctantly left her sister in the capable hands of victim support.

HE MOTIONED her to the only soft chair in his office. "Please, take a seat."

She did as she was told.

Llewellyn drew his swivel chair alongside. "How are you feeling? I hear you signed yourself out of hospital last night."

She looked down at her skirt, smoothing it with her hands. "I didn't *need* to be in hospital, sir."

"They wanted to keep you in for observation."

"Seriously, I didn't need it."

"Are you fit for work?"

"Yes. Yes, of course."

He placed his hand under her chin, turning her face towards his. "Forgive me, I need to see for myself." He took his hand away again. "You look exhausted, Yvonne. More tired than I have ever seen you. What happened?"

"It was my surveillance area. I took my eye off the ball. I-"

"No." He shook his head. "I meant, what caused the collapse?"

"I had a panic attack." Her gaze was once more on her skirt. She felt ashamed.

"Do you need more counselling?"

Her face flew to his and she bit her lip. "They're my nephew and niece. I haven't had a panic attack for six months. I had one last night because I was scared for the children. I'm their aunty. Surely, I'm allowed that?"

He nodded. "Nonetheless, I'm referring you to occupational health. I hope you understand."

"So, can I carry on working in the meantime?" She searched his face.

"You can, but..." He sighed, his eyes moving from side-to-side, as though looking for the right words. "You can no longer be involved in this case."

"What?" She stared at him, open-mouthed.

"You're too close, Yvonne. You know you are. What would you do in my shoes? What would you do if it were Dewi, or Callum, or Dai?"

She bowed her head again.

"You know I'm right, Yvonne." He put a hand on her arm. "For the sake of your health, your sanity, and this case, I'm asking you to take a week's leave. Please do so."

"You do know that my sister is staying with me?" Her eyes sparked with a frustration only just held in check.

"Yes, I do. And that's fine. You'll be kept up to date, in any event. We wouldn't leave you in the dark. Get some rest." His eyes were gentle, as he rose and held the door open for her. "You'll be back before you know it." He smiled. "You'd better be. You're my best officer and I'll be lost without you."

25

HELLISH NIGHT

It had been several days since Kyle had last eaten. He was drinking, but not nearly enough. Donna was beside herself with worry and Peter was struggling to help her. He was angry, every so often, kicking out at walls and doors.

They received little communication from their captors. Ordinarily, Donna would have been fine with that. But, with Kyle becoming more sick, the situation was becoming more desperate.

"Where are the police? What's taking them so long?" Peter sat on the edge of the bed, arms folded. "They track everyone these days, don't they? Why don't they know where we are?"

Donna walked over to the door. "Help," she called. "We need a doctor."

To their surprise, they heard keys in the lock. A masked man pushed water and soup, on a tray, through the door and was about to close it again.

"Wait, don't go," Donna begged.

Peter put his foot in the door.

The other man kicked at the foot to remove it. He said nothing to the youngsters, but he didn't leave right away.

"Move back into the room, Peter," Donna ordered. "Do it now, please."

Peter paused, fists clenched.

"Please? For Kyle's sake?"

He backed up, glowering at the masked man.

"Look," Donna pointed. "It's Kyle. Over there, on the bed. He's not eating and he has a fever. He's had the fever for at least two days. He needs medical help."

The man nodded and left, once again locking them in.

Half-an-hour later, he was back, pushing a bottle of Calpol into the room.

Donna got up to go and talk to the him but the door was already locked again.

"Wait, he's not eating-" She dropped back, deflated.

Kyle murmured in his sleep.

"Shall we give him some of this?" Peter held up the Calpol.

Donna nodded. "I'll do it and I'll try to get some of the soup and water down him. Then, we should all get some sleep."

THEY HAD BARELY SLEPT, when the door was unlocked once more. Two small children were pushed into the room. The little boy held a working torch. The little girl was crying.

Donna sat bolt upright, heart beating fast after her sudden awakening. The light from the torch hurt her eyes.

"Can I have that?" She tried to extract the flashlight from the little boy, but he resisted. "Please? My name is Donna and I'd just like to see who you are."

Reluctantly, Tom gave up the torch.

Donna pointed it at the wall, using the reflected light to look at the small children.

"What's going on?" Peter pushed himself up. As he did so, Kyle rolled over into the space he had vacated and continued sleeping.

"I'm sorry you've been brought here in the middle of the night." She passed the torch to Peter. "Can you hold this for me? These children have just been pushed in here." She turned her attention back to the little ones. "What are your names?"

"Tom. Can I have my torch back now?" He held out his hand.

"In a minute." Donna rubbed her hand in his hair. "And who's this?" She bent her head to Sally, who had stopped crying and wiped her nose with her sleeve.

"Sally." Tom answered for her. "She's my sister."

"Well, hello Tom and Sally. It's nice to meet you. I'm Donna and this is Peter and Kyle. Kyle is fast asleep. He's a little bit poorly. How old are you?"

"Six," Tom answered, confidently.

"Seven." Sally averted her gaze, her posture awkward.

Tom walked right up to the older girl. "Where's my mummy?"

"Yes, where is she?" Sally moved closer to her brother.

Donna cleared her throat. "She's been held up. I think she'll be here before long."

"I want her now." Sally began to cry again.

"I know you do, sweetheart." Donna scooped her up.

"It's so dark in here and I'm cold. I want go home." Sally burrowed into Donna.

"Come on under this blanket. We'll get you warm."

"I'll sleep across the bottom of the bed," Peter said, getting out to make room.

"Thank you." Donna gave his hand a squeeze as he passed.

~

Kim had had her first sleep since the children went missing. It had lasted only three hours but Yvonne was glad that her sister had finally gotten some rest. She heard her padding downstairs to the kitchen and checked the clock. Six-thirty am, and the beginning of her second day away from the station. It didn't feel right. It felt even less right, because Kim, Tom and Sally needed her. She jumped out of bed to take a shower.

The smell of coffee wafted up the stairs. It smelled good. She ran down to join Kim in the kitchen, just as the percolator finished doing its work.

"That was good timing." Kim poured milk into a jug.

"How are you?" Yvonne put a hand on Kim's shoulder.

Kim turned to her, eyes still rimmed with red and with a haunted look in her thinning face. She shook her head.

"Have something to eat, please. You haven't eaten anything properly in three days. We can't have you collapsing. You have to stay strong for the children. They are going to need you in good health when they return home."

"What if they don't return home?" Kim's eyes returned to the DI's face. "I can't help going there in my head. What if they don't come home?"

"Hey, hey. Don't think like that. There are so many people, police and intelligence units working on this. There's some really good people involved. They think they know who took the children and, as far as we know, this group has not harmed any of the children they have taken. They've just used their pictures to make demands."

"So, they'll do the same with Sally and Tom?"

"I'm expecting something to come out any day now, Kim. Yes."

"The hackers and the Go-Fund-Me things that were on the news? Is that what you were working on, on your birthday?"

Yvonne sighed. "We had set up a sting ready for if an attempted abduction took place, yes. We had intel to suggest it would."

"And I took my children right into the trap."

"You weren't to know that, Kim."

"Why didn't you tell me what you were working on?"

"I couldn't, Kim. You know that. This case was… *is* very sensitive. If the kidnappers get wind of the sting, they don't show up and then, we're no further forward."

Kim passed Yvonne a mug of coffee and the jug of milk. "I'm sorry. I'm not blaming you. I chose to bring the children to you. I actually didn't know you would be at the fair. I had thought I would take the children there and message you, asking you what time you finished. We hadn't long arrived when I spotted you walking and decided to spring the surprise. I still can't get my head around my children being taken so quickly." Kim's eyes were full again.

"It's frustrating that I have been taken off this. There's so much I wanted to do. I was working some strong leads, when Llewellyn pulled me. I'm tempted to continue with them under the radar, but, in no way do I want to jeopardise yours, or any of the other children."

Kim's eyes showed a spark of life. "I could help you. I could help you work your leads."

"I don't think that would be a good idea, Kim. But I have asked one of my best friends, who also happens to be a criminal psychologist, to go over things with me. I may not be able to work the case directly, but I have no doubt that we'll be able to feed in ideas to Dewi and the team. I just need to be very careful and thoroughly think things through."

~

YVONNE SWALLOWED HARD, remote in hand. She looked across at her sister.

"It's okay. Go ahead. I'd rather know," Kim reassured.

She pressed the red button and the TV fired into life. The lunchtime news was about to start.

As expected, the major headline and first news item was about the extortion group. Vortex had released another of their videos, demanding Bitcoin. The BBC was refusing to show the video. Yvonne had to hunt it down on her laptop.

'We warned you what would happen.' The voice, as usual, was computer-generated. 'You don't meet our demands, we take more children and look what we have here.'

The screen went from pitch black to two small children sitting on high stools, in the bright glare of a overhead spotlights. Both of them were crying and Tom was calling for his mum.

"Bastards!" Yvonne clenched her fists, fear and anger coursing through every fibre. She turned to Kim, who ran to press her hand against the TV and the images of her children, tears streaming down her face.

Yvonne ran to her and, as the video ended, she held her sister until the sobs subsided, more determined than ever to catch the culprits and get have them punished.

26

TASHA

Her knocks on the front door having gone unanswered, Tasha put her bags down and tried the handle. The door was open. As she went through to the lounge, it was obvious why they had not heard her. Yvonne and Kim were in the middle of a brainstorming session. Pieces of paper and sticky notes littered the coffee table and it was clear from the numerous brown rings on them that the sisters were surviving on caffeine.

"Tasha!" Yvonne stood up and ran over to greet her friend. "I'm so glad you're here. Come and meet my sister, Kim. She's been helping me work through my ideas."

"Nice to meet you. I've heard a lot about you." Tasha could see the resemblance between them. They had the same nose and eyes. The same shaped face. Different hair colour. Kim was much darker. She gave the latter a hug and felt Kim's thin frailty, through her loose-hanging clothes. "I am so sorry for what has happened."

"Can you help us?" Kim searched Tasha's face.

Tasha's heart went out to her, and the unspeakable pain

lurking in those half-lidded, sunken eyes. "I'll give it my best shot."

Yvonne reached out to take hold of the psychologist's bags. "I'll take these through to your room, and I'll show you what I have been working on. I've been taken off the case."

"Of course." Tasha nodded. "There isn't a force in the country that would allow you to work a case in which your own relatives are involved."

Yvonne placed Tasha's things in the guest room, and turned to her friend. "But, I'm close. I know it. I just can't quite put the pieces together."

Tasha put a hand on her shoulder, giving it a squeeze. "That's because so much is riding on it and the fear for your nephew and niece will stop you thinking clearly."

∽

Yvonne felt that she had gone through everything she could think of with Tasha. The coffee table was littered with even more paper.

Tasha pursed her lips. "Carantan is an interesting character. His reaction to you in interview and the possibility of his having had a relationship with a member of his team, who just then happens to fall off a cliff."

"What if he is the mastermind behind Vortex?" Yvonne sat back, rubbing her lips, distractedly.

"He sounds shady as hell, but that doesn't necessarily add up to being behind Vortex."

"No, I know." The DI snapped forward. "But, I think it too much of a coincidence that his flat, and his dead ex-colleague or lover, are used to register a vehicle involved in at least one of the abductions."

"I see your point." Tasha pursed her lips. "So, what's your next move?"

"I've got his address. He lives near Talybont. Will you come with me on a stakeout?"

"Tasha frowned. "On a stakeout? Are you mad? You're officially off the case. It could blow up on you."

Yvonne sighed. "I know. Look, if we find anything, I will report it immediately to Llewellyn, okay? We will not make a move ourselves. We just go up there, and observe for a bit. Watch him come and go."

Tasha scratched her chin, lips in a tight line.

"What if the children are being held at his house? In a basement or something? Remember the sadist?"

"Even more reason why this should be done by a team with full back-up, Yvonne."

The DI nodded. "I know... I just feel... helpless." Her shoulders dropped, along with the corners of her mouth. She looked years older.

Tasha relented. "Okay. What harm can it do? We can take my car and observe his comings and goings. We'll stock up on sandwiches and coffee and watch from a safe distance. If we see anything concerning or suspicious, you call it in. Even if it's just a call to Dewi for him to check it out. Agreed?"

Yvonne nodded, the light returning to her eyes. "Agreed."

∼

A LIGHT FROST had rendered the world pale, around them. They were twenty minutes into the journey to Talybont, in Tasha's Mazda. The sky was a delicate shade of blue and a light mist rose from the grasslands, as the frost evaporated in the sun's rays.

Yvonne's mobile made her jump. It was Dewi.

"Ma'am, just calling to see how you are and let you know how we're doing."

A smile relaxed her face. "Dewi, it's great to hear from you. I'm with Tasha. We're on our way to Talybont."

Tasha shot her a stern look.

Yvonne shrugged, her hand over the phone. "It's okay, it's Dewi."

"I know who it is." Tasha frowned. "But-"

"You're on your way to Talybont? What are you going to do there?"

"Just a bit of observation, nothing strenuous."

There was a moments silence. "Wait a minute, isn't that where Carl Carantan lives? What are you up to?"

"Is anyone with you?"

"No. I'm on my own."

"Okay, good. Look, I've been thinking that all roads lead to Carantan, so we are off up there to stake him out for a bit. See what he gets up to."

"What if he spots you?"

"Hopefully, he won't. And if he does, I'll deal with that when it comes to it. I'm a police officer, it's what we do."

"You're off the case, ma'am. This is risky in more ways than one." Dewi had lowered his voice. "You could be disciplined, even suspended for this."

Yvonne sighed. "Dewi, my nephew and niece are being held hostage-"

"That's the whole point. You're not in your right mind. Look, where are you now?"

"About twenty-five minutes from Talybont."

"Pull over in a lay-by and wait for me. I'm on my way. If

you're going to do this, at least have an officer with you who is on active duty."

Yvonne grinned. "Thank you, Dewi."

"What car you in?"

"A red Mazda."

"A red Mazda? Well, you're not going to stick out in *that* now, are you?"

"Are you coming or not?"

"Give me fifteen to twenty minutes and I'll be there. Don't move," he ordered.

"Yes, sir."

WHILE THEY WAITED, Yvonne put a quick call in to Kim to check she was all right. She had wanted to stay by the phone and where she could easily access the news. She knew she could call if there were any concerns.

When Dewi caught up with them, he suggested Tasha leave her car in the village and he drove them in his black Astra.

They found a location above Carantan's house, where they could observe him coming and going, through the gaps in a convenient farm gate. They did not have to wait long.

Carantan parked his car in the tarmac yard, in front of his house. Dewi passed his binoculars to Yvonne, whilst he viewed through an SLR camera and zoom lens.

Carantan got out of his car and checked right and left, before opening the boot. The DI held her breath.

He pulled out a box, resting it on the top of his car, whilst he closed and locked the car. His knees bent, he carried the box with both arms to the foot of his garage. The garage was unlocked. He pulled it open and lifted the box to take it inside.

That done, he walked back to his car and drove away.

Yvonne looked at Dewi. "I didn't see him lock the garage."

Dewi bit the inside of his cheek.

"Come on, Dewi. Did you see how furtive he looked before he took that box out of the boot? There's something in it, I know it."

"What if he comes back?" Tasha asked, from the back seat.

"He's most likely gone back to work. Mike told me he comes and goes a lot. He's up to something." Yvonne opened the passenger door.

"Come on." Dewi grabbed his tweed jacket from behind his seat. "Five minutes. Let's go. Sorry, Tasha. You'll have to stay here, I'm afraid."

Tahsa nodded. "No worries. I'll borrow the binoculars."

Yvonne and Dewi ran down through the field at the back of the house.

"I'll knock on the front door, in case somebody is home," Dewi shouted back to Yvonne, who smiled to herself. It was very strange not being in the driving seat for once.

When there was no answer, and after Yvonne had scraped loose mud clumps from her trainers, they headed for the garage.

Dewi tried it and it opened easily. The DI followed him inside.

Carantan's garage was just like any other. There were work benches along three walls with various bits and pieces, mostly tools, on them and tools hanging on the wall. On the bench furthest away from them, they could see the box he had taken from his boot.

Yvonne crossed over to it. "It's not taped up. That's going to make it a bit easier."

Dewi paused. "Perhaps there nothing important in it? This could be a wasted mission."

Yvonne tutted. "Nothing is ever wasted, Dewi. Nothing is ever wasted."

Taking care, she opened the box flaps. Although their eyes had adjusted, the light from the open garage door was not enough. Yvonne grabbed a torch from the workbench and Dewi closed the garage door behind them.

Yvonne stared open-mouthed at the contents. "Wow. This is not what I expected to find." She began sifting through the contents and taking one or two pieces out.

"Photographs?" Dewi looked at Yvonne.

Yvonne held up one of the frames. It was a photograph of Carantan staring into the eyes of another, younger, male. She was surprised at the tenderness she saw in Carantan's gaze. She turned it over. "He's written on the back, Dewi. Look."

"'Mathew. Clarach Bay, 2015.' It's Mathew Hinds. They were having a relationship. He *was* seeing him." Her eyes flicked from side-to-side, as she thought this through.

There were more photographs of Carantan and Mathew. A ring, some books, evidently given to Carantan by Mathew, as he had written messages in the front.

Yvonne read aloud. "'To Carl, from Mathew H. Christmas 2014.'"

"Sad memorabilia." Dewi sighed.

"Wait, what's this?" Yvonne pulled out a group photograph, obviously taken at the university campus and showing Carantan fronting a small group. She flipped it over.

"Research group. Summer. 2014," she read. "Look, there's Mathew, and that guy there," she pointed at a young man standing next to Carantan, "is Mike Jones, who I have spoken to a couple of times."

"He's the one I saw you speak to at the library."

"That's right. Wait. Wait a minute, Dewi. Do you recognise that guy? What's he doing in the photo?"

"Which guy?" Dewi peered at the face she was pointing to. "That's-"

"Joe Benton, isn't it?"

"My thoughts exactly." Deep lines appeared on her forehead.

"What's that?" Dewi put a hand out. "I can hear a car," he whispered.

Yvonne held her breath. The sound of a car door banging shut outside had her heart pounding hard. She licked her lips and shot a look towards Dewi.

They couldn't run for it. All they could do was hope that it wasn't Carantan, or that, if it was, he didn't head straight for the garage.

The garage door lifted up, leaving them both blinking as the bright sunlight flooded in.

"What the bloody hell are you doing in my garage?" Carantan's silhouette shouted at them. "You'd better be in possession of a warrant."

"We are." Dewi reached into his jacket pocket and held aloft a folded piece of paper.

Carantan moved further into the garage and, as their eyes adjusted, they could see the worry on his face.

"We're sorry, Doctor Carantan. We did knock on your door, but you weren't in."

"I went to get some milk from the village. Anyway, I have to go back to work in an hour."

"Sure." Yvonne cleared her throat, looking towards the box.

"You've been going through my stuff?" Carantan swallowed hard.

"We looked through the box, yes. Why didn't you tell me you were having a relationship with Mathew, before he died?"

"You'd have accused me of having something to do with his death." Carantan had the look of a defeated man.

"Did you?" Her gaze was direct.

"No, of course, not." He sighed. "Whatever you may think of me, I loved Mathew. He meant the world to me. Yes, I was the research leader. Yes, I was married and not ready to give up on myself and Marian, but I loved him. And, he could make up his own mind who he wanted to see. He wasn't a boy. He was a twenty-five year old post-doc, more than capable of making his own decisions."

"Did he threaten to tell your wife? Is that why you killed him?" Dewi put both hands on his hips.

"What?" Carantan stared at Dewi, open-mouthed. "No. He did not. He wouldn't have done that. *I* wouldn't have done that. What we had was special. Hence the box." He walked towards it, taking a sideways glance at Yvonne. "After he died, I couldn't bear to part with these things. I couldn't keep them here. I couldn't risk Marian finding them." He sighed. "She's left, by the way. Left me two days ago." He ran his hand over the photographs in the box. "I kept these in the loft at the top of the flats. When you came to see me about the vehicle that you said had been registered to one of my flats, I took them out of there, in case you went poking around."

"I see." Yvonne felt for him in a way she hadn't expected to. She understood.

"You took them out because you knew we would suspect you of being involved in his death." Dewi hadn't given up.

Carantan ran both hands through his hair. "Really," he sighed. "I loved him. I did not harm him. But, I did blame myself for his death for a long time. He had wanted me to leave Marian and I had had neither the courage, nor the sense of purpose, to do it. I thought perhaps he had ended it all because he didn't see a future for us."

"And now?" Yvonne asked in soft voice.

"Now, I don't believe that. He knew how much I cared about him. I no longer think he killed himself because of me."

Yvonne joined him at the box and pulled out the research group photograph. "Can I ask you about this man?" She pointed to Joe Benton.

Carantan peered at the photograph. "That's Joseph Benton. He was a postgraduate student with me. He dropped out, before finishing. Why do you ask?"

"Do you know why he dropped out?" Yvonne asked.

Carantan screwed up his nose in thought. "If I remember rightly, he left a couple of weeks after Mathew's death. I think he couldn't deal with it. Doing a PhD is stressful enough, without one of your colleagues and friends committing suicide."

"Did you ever speak to him again, after he left?"

"No. No, he didn't get in touch. I wrote to him. He had been so close to finishing, I offered for him to come back and continue. I didn't get a reply."

"Thank you, Doctor Carantan. And, I am sorry about Mathew. I am really sorry for your loss." Her soulful eyes would leave Carantan in no doubt that she meant it.

∽

"BENTON," Yvonne muttered, as they left Carantan's house.

"I don't know why I didn't think of it before. Lisa told us he had dropped out of university. I didn't think to enquire further."

"Well, why would you?" Dewi held the gate open for her.

She raised an eyebrow at him. "By the way, how did you get that warrant so fast?"

Dewi chuckled. "I didn't." He held up the folded paper. "This is a delivery note."

Yvonne laughed, giving him a friendly rap on the shoulder. "Good grief, you're getting as bad as me."

27

GETTING CLOSE?

Yvonne accepted the glass of wine from Tasha, appreciating the logs crackling in the fireplace. Not for the first time, she rubbed her hands together.

"Warming up now?" Tasha held out the red-checked woollen blanket she had taken from the back of the sofa.

Yvonne nodded. "Loving this fire."

Tasha smiled. "Knew you would."

Yvonne reached for her phone. "No messages."

"Nothing at all?" Tasha tilted her head to one side.

"Not yet." The DI pursed her lips. "They should be there, already. I'm sure Dewi will get in touch as soon as he can, depending on whether Benton is being difficult."

A cry came upstairs.

Yvonne stilled, tilting her head to listen. "That's Kim. I'll go check on her."

"Would you like me to come?" Tasha moved forward on the sofa.

Yvonne shook her head. "No, it's okay."

Kim was fast asleep, only her second proper sleep since

the children were taken. Sweat-soaked, her hair clung to her forehead and streaked across her cheek. She cried out again. "No, No." Her head thrashed about on the damp pillow.

Yvonne placed a cooling hand on her sister's brow. Even in sleep, this had a calming effect and Kim's head stopped thrashing. The DI waited for her sister's sleep to deepen again, before heading back down to the lounge.

"She was having a nightmare." Yvonne sighed, as she sat back down. "If anything happens today, and I have to go, will you stay with her?"

Tasha nodded. "Of course. I'll take care of her. You won't need to worry."

∼

Dewi knocked on DCI Llewellyn's door and went straight in.

"Sir, we want to raid a property in Llanidloes, in connection with the child abductions. We'll need uniform, a dog team and an ARV on standby."

"Wow." Llewellyn got up from behind desk. "Who's the suspect?"

"A Mr Joseph Benton. We're not sure how, yet, but we believe he's involved with the IT input for the kidnappers, and maybe even more."

"Okay, well, bring him in. I'll call for the backup teams and you can ready yourself. Take Callum."

"We don't have enough to charge him, but I'm hoping his computers and phone will fill in the gaps. We also think he could be involved in a suspicious death, three years ago. I'd like to question him about that."

Llewellyn nodded. "Are you saying you only have circumstantial evidence at the moment?"

"That's right. He seems to link in all over the place. Like a linchpin."

"Okay, take it steady and keep me informed. I want him charged or let go within seventy-two hours."

∼

Frost had already begun to coat the hedges and grass lawns. It sparkled in the streetlights, as Dewi and Callum arrived at the black-and-white, three-storey house with the green door. Callum knocked with force. "Police. Police, open up!"

No answer.

"Police. Open the door."

Still no answer. Dewi bent his head forward, straining to listen.

A shout went up from one of the PCs who had gone around the back.

"What did he say?" Dewi asked.

"I think Benton has gone out the back." Callum made his way back down the path.

One of the officers ran back around to him. "He's climbed out the bloody window. He's running hell for leather through the neighbour's gardens. Three officers have gone after him."

"Thanks." Dewi ran towards one of the vehicles, shouting at the occupants. "We'll need your dogs. He's made a run for it."

Benton kept running, over the bridge to the river, followed by several officers. He was described over the radio as wearing dark clothing and his hood was up.

Dewi paused to catch his breath. "You go," he said between gasps. "I'll catch you up." He bent almost double, in an effort to get his breath back. He saw something glinting in the light from streetlamp. Bending down, he could see it was a sim card in a ziplock sandwich bag. He picked it up.

Callum continued running. Despite his smoking habit, he was proud of his fitness. He checked for his cuffs in his left jacket pocket, just in case, and paused on the river path to get his bearings.

Two officers with dogs combed the bank, while the rest of them spread out, torches lighting up the foliage and water in waves.

Dewi put a call in to the DCI and let him know what was happening, reassuring him that they would not be needing the armed response unit. He walked quickly for the rest of the way, one hand supporting his lower back, the sim card package safely in his jacket pocket.

~

THE DOGS BARKED IN UNISON, straining on their leashes. Down in the water, clinging to a large tree root, Benton shivered in the torchlight. Callum ran to help a PC pull him out. Their quarry offered no resistance, the spirit-sapping cold had done its work.

Callum palmed his cuffs and placed them on the dripping-wet Benton, in the front stack position. "Joseph Benton. I am arresting you on suspicion of conspiracy to kidnap. You do not have to say anything, but it may harm your defence if you do not mention, when questioned, something which you later rely on in court. Anything you do say will be given in evidence."

Dewi arrived as Benton was being led along the path.

Head bowed, the prisoner said nothing. He said nothing, either, as he was caged in the back of the van, blanket wrapped around his shoulders. Neither did he speak when he was booked into custody, searched and taken to a cell where his belt and laces were removed.

Uniform officers booked Benton's laptop, an iPad and two mobile phones into evidence, ready for the lab.

DCI Llewellyn appeared ecstatic. "Good work, boys. I'll put in a call to George Lucas. Let him know we've got the suspect's tech. Take the lad a hot soup and get him dried out ready for interview."

"Sir." Dewi held up his hand. "There's one more thing. I found a discarded sim. I can't say for sure, but I think Benton threw it away during the chase. I think the lab should take a look at it. It's booked into evidence."

Llewellyn placed both hands on his hips. It was almost a superhero pose. "Well, this just gets better. We'll need to let Lucas know about that, too." His grin could not have been any wider. He loosened his tie. "Well done, indeed."

~

SULLEN-FACED AND UNSHAVEN, Benton sat with his arms folded, in a white paper suit. He was joined by a duty solicitor, who kept checking his watch and sighing every few minutes. Dewi introduced everyone for the purpose of the recording. He and Callum took their positions on the opposite side of the table.

Dewi kicked off with the caution reminder. "Joseph Benton, I would like to remind you that you are still under caution. If you fail to mention anything *now*, which you later rely on in court, it could harm your defence."

Benton stared angrily at Dewi. "I've got nothing to say to you." His gaze lowered to the table.

Dewi leaned back in his chair, both hands in his trouser

pockets. "You're facing some potentially very serious charges, Joseph." He pursed his lips. "If they find what I think they'll find on your laptop and...sim card-"

Benton's head flicked up, his eyes wider than before. "There's nothing on them." The words were thrown out like punches. Benton's face flushed. He folded his arms, gaze returning to the table.

"You know that SOCA are involved. That's the Serious and Organised-"

"I know what it is," Benton spat.

Dewi nodded. "So, tell us what you know. Are you the ring leader?"

Benton shifted in his chair, flicking his head every so often, as though his thoughts were erratically changing direction. "I don't know what you're talking about."

"Ever heard of Vortex?"

"Leading question," the solicitor accused.

"Tell us who your friends are. Who do you talk to on social media?"

"No comment."

"Children are being kept away from their families. Scared and probably cold. Can you live with that?"

"No comment."

Dewi sighed. "Perhaps you need time to think about things. I tell you what. We'll leave you for a little while. Let you think about the possible consequences of your actions. Is that okay?"

"No comment."

"Very well." Dewi scraped his chair backwards and stood, quickly followed by Callum.

Benton's solicitor followed them outside. "You haven't got anything, have you? If you've got any evidence, charge him. If not, you have to let him go."

Dewi's eyes bored into the solicitor. "He ran from us. We knocked on his door and he ran. He discarded a sim card. We may not have all the answers right now, but; we will. And in the meantime, he stays where he is."

Dewi's mobile vibrated in his pocket.

"Dewi Hughes."

"Dewi, it's Yvonne. What's happening?"

Dewi filled her in.

"Is Benton still there?"

"Yeah. Solicitor's putting pressure on us to let him go but we've still got him at the moment."

"Good. I'll speak to Llewellyn. I have to come back."

28

PERSUASION

Yvonne dialled Llewellyn's number and held her breath.

"DCI Llewellyn?" His voice was slow and low-pitched. Tired.

"Sir, it's Yvonne."

"Yvonne, how are you?" His pitch lifted a little.

"I'm okay. I want to come back." There was no time to beat around the bush.

"I'm sorry, Yvonne. You can't do that. You're too close."

"You're not getting anywhere with Benton."

"How do you know that?" His voice was clipped.

"Er... I just do. Let me talk to him."

"Yvonne-"

"Look, if Benton is connected to Vortex, then the longer he stays out of touch, the more suspicious and on edge they are going to get. If he is due to make a call to them and he misses it? Those children... We could face the worst case scenario. We can't let that happen. We have to move."

"Well, I-"

"Please, sir. Let me talk to him. Let me *at least* try."

"What about SOCA. They won't be happy."

"Do they know my nephew and niece are victims?"

"Not yet."

"Then don't tell them."

"They're going to find out."

"They don't know *now*."

Llewellyn sighed. "All right. All right. When can you get here?"

"I'll be there in twenty minutes."

∼

Callum and Dewi were having coffee when Yvonne arrived. Callum excused himself, desperate for a cigarette.

"Has he talked yet?" She breathed heavily, after running up the stairs.

"No. He's not budging." Dewi eyed her, his expression gentle. "Sure you're okay to do this?"

She nodded. "I just hope I can make a difference. Are his computers with the lab?"

"They are. It's taking a while to crack them. He's clearly super-cautious. That tells me he is *definitely* hiding something."

"Okay, well, let's go see if we can find out what that is."

For the purposes of the recording, Dewi introduced himself again, as he entered the room.

"DI Yvonne Giles. Hello, Joseph. Do you remember me?"

Benton stared at her.

She noticed he had picked a hole in the knee of his paper suit.

"I hear you had a dip in the river," she continued. "That must have been cold. I hope you've warmed up a little now."

Benton looked down at his thighs.

"Would you like a coffee?"

Benton nodded, still looking down.

"Do you have milk and sugar?"

He nodded again. "Three sugars."

Yvonne got up to request the coffee from the PC on the other side of the interview room door.

"It'll be here in a few minutes." She returned to her seat. "Joseph, I wanted to ask you if you know anything about an organisation calling themselves Vortex? Does that name ring a bell?"

Benton remained silent, his eyes flicking up to the clock.

"See, I think you do. I think you have been helping them." She sat back in her chair, rubbing her chin with slow, deliberate movements. "I ask myself why someone, with such a promising career in computer science, would be living in a run-down house and working in a supermarket. And, taking in others who have walked out on their lives. Youngsters who have abandoned everything, just as you did."

Benton locked eyes with her.

"Yes, I know that you had almost qualified with your PhD when you left Aberystwyth University. So close... You had almost completed your thesis. Why, Joseph? why did you give up?"

Benton shook his head. "I didn't want it any more. I wasn't the first student to drop out. It happens all the time."

"You were one of a bunch of very gifted young men." She leaned in towards him. "Did something happen? Did something happen to make you want to leave so suddenly?"

He backed away from her. "No."

"Who were your friends at college? Who did you hang around with?"

Benton was silent.

"I know that you were working in Carl Carantan's research group. You were working with Mathew Hinds and Mike Jones."

He opened his mouth, as though about to say something, but closed it again.

"How well did you know Mathew Hinds?"

He chewed the inside of his cheek.

"You left within weeks of him falling off that cliff."

He cleared his throat and folded his arms across his chest.

"What happened, Joseph? What happened to Mathew? Did someone cause his fall."

"Wait a minute, what is this?" The solicitor held up his hand. "This is supposed to be about Joseph's potential connection to Vortex. Are you now looking at him for causing a death?"

"I promise you, this is all part of the same enquiry." Yvonne's voice was soft. She turned back to Benton. "You see, I don't think *you* would have caused Mathew's death. You abandoned your career and spent your time rescuing others. That doesn't sound to me like someone who would ruthlessly take another's life. No, if someone pushed Mathew off that cliff, they had far less empathy than that. They would have gone on to continue building their career, no matter what? Am I right?"

Benton was still chewing his cheek.

"But, you couldn't, could you? You couldn't live with what happened, so you left."

"Mathew Hinds committed suicide." Benton put his head in his hands.

"Did he? Is that what happened?"

Yvonne placed a photograph on the table. "For the tape, I am showing Mr Benton a photograph of himself and others, including Carl Carantan, Mathew Hinds and Mike Jones."

Benton stared at the photograph. A tear dripped onto it.

"What happened to Mathew? Were you there?"

Benton wiped his eyes with one of his paper sleeves.

"The suicide verdict was changed to one of open verdict. The coroner noted marks on Mathew which were not consistent with the fall from the cliff. Those marks were extra, and caused prior to his death. Any ideas how those marks got there? Was anyone fighting with Mathew, prior to his death? Did *you* fight with him? Was it over a girl?"

"You don't know what you're talking about!" Mathew blurted the words, saliva bursting forth from between his lips and mucous streaming from his nose. "I tried to warn Mathew. I told him to keep out of it. I told him to let it go." He shook his head. "He didn't listen to me."

"Told him to let what go?"

"We used his ideas to get money. I had debts. I just wanted to pay those off but..." Benton fell silent.

"But what? Who else was involved in making money? Joseph?"

"I need the toilet."

"Really?"

"Really."

"Interview paused, seven-ten pm."

∽

CARANTAN AMBLED THROUGH THE HALL. His body hunched, he lifted his scarf from the coat stand and wound it around his neck til it felt secure. He checked his watch. Six o'clock. Mike would be there any minute.

Words and scenarios burrowed through his brain like

woodworm. And, if he closed his eyes, he could still see Mathew saying goodbye for one last time. His smile, open and care-free. Only now, the image of that smile turned into a grimace of pain and fear.

What had Mathew felt, before being launched off that lonely clifftop? Had he looked around for help, only to find there was none? The town below, settling into its evening routine, would be blissfully unaware of the horror unfolding.

The doorbell made him jump. Mike.

Carantan inhaled a deep lungful of air and opened the door.

Mike looked smart in his dark jeans, crisp, cotton shirt and long, black coat. He had tamed his hair with gel and was smiling, with that extrovert confidence of the young and beautiful.

"Ready?" Mike held out an arm.

Carantan looked down at it, before sliding his through. In his head, it was like linking with barbed wire.

"The hill is quiet, Carl. Just how we like it."

Carantan nodded, his breath wisping out through his nose, in the darkness. "It was a night just like this."

"Sorry?" Mike turned to look at him.

Carantan shook his head. "Nothing. Are we going?"

"Jump in." They reached Mike's battered vehicle and Mike ran around to the driver's side. There was an excitement in his step. It turned Carantan's gut.

"You're quiet," Mike accused, eyes straight ahead as he fired up the engine ready for the drive to Aberystwyth. "Are you pining for Marian? She'll probably come back, you know."

Carantan pursed his lips.

"Seriously," Mike gave a laugh, "if you're going to be like

this, we may as well knock our walk on the head." He paused from pulling out of the drive.

That was not what Carantan wanted. Sighing, he brushed his trouser legs as though wiping them free of crumbs. "Sorry, Mike. Just a bit distracted, that's all. It's been a strange week."

"You said the police had been to see you." Mike shot a sideways glance at him. "What did they want?" His knuckles tightened around the steering wheel.

Carantan rubbed his eyes. "They're working on a cold case. They thought one of their suspects might have lived at the flats."

"Oh, I see."

They drove the rest of the twelve-mile journey in silence, save for the whirring of the engine and occasional tic-toc of the indicators.

Mike parked in a tiny lay-by, at the back of the buildings fronting the Aberystwyth promenade, at the foot of Constitution Hill.

This was the least furtive they had been. Carantan, though tense, was more relaxed than he would have been two weeks ago. Whatever their differences, he would not have wanted Marian to find out from gossip. He *had* loved her. Still did, in his own way. He sighed, stepping out into the cold night air.

"Something's wrong. I know it is." Mike refrained from touch this time, merely walking beside Carantan as a friend might.

The sound of the sea's rhythmic bathing of the shore was the only accompaniment as they began the winding walk up the hill. This place had always provided the solitude and privacy they craved. Tonight, there was something else. Something he couldn't quite put his finger on. They were a little out of breath when they reached the top, taking a moment to get it back. They reached the flat courtyard of the red-roofed cafe and could see the closed office at the start of the funicular railway, the tracks of which, ran down to where the car was parked.

Mike took hold of Carantan's hand and was surprised at its coldness. They stood, looking down at the town nestled below them, curving round the bay from Constitution Hill to the university's Old College and on, to the castle and monument. A few dog walkers and the odd couple on the beaches below were highlighted in the headlights of passing cars. Everything appeared tiny from up there. A miniature world beneath their feet.

"What are you thinking?" Mike turned to Carantan. He moved his head to kiss him. Carantan pulled back. The movement was minute, but enough to stop Mike in his tracks. "Carl?"

"This is one of the last sights Mathew had," Carantan said, still gazing down at the town." He turned to Mike. "But, it wasn't quite the last." He walked swiftly to his right, heading towards a small bench and the twenty-pence telescope, several feet from the sheer drop off the cliff.

Mike swallowed hard.

"This was the last. The *very* last."

~

"Interview resumed, seven-thirty pm. What did you warn Mathew about, Joseph?"

Benton sighed. "Mathew had been working on some code. A zero-day exploit, that allowed access to large computer networks. It was undetectable and untraceable, unless you knew what you were looking for. He wasn't intending to use it for anything illegal. He just wanted to prove he could do it."

"Okay... What happened then? Did someone else use that code?"

"Yes. We got hold of the code and used it to gain access to a banking network and creamed off small amounts from a lot of accounts. Kind of like getting access to a vault full of deposit boxes, except this was all online."

"Who's we? Who else was involved?"

Benton appeared not to have heard her. "Mathew found out and went ballistic. He said he was going to the police. We asked him to go for a walk with us. Hear us out. Think things through."

"Who's us, Joseph?"

"I never went up there with the intention of Mathew getting hurt and I would *never* have wanted to cause his death." Joseph broke down. "I had nothing to do with what happened."

"Joseph, who else was involved?"

Joseph put his head back in his hands. He no longer made any attempt to stop or wipe away his tears. "Mike. It was Mike's idea to use the code. He asked me to help him. I should have said no. I had debts. I owed rent and needed money for food. We used the code to hack a major bank. We were never caught."

"What happened, the night Mathew died?"

"Mike spoke to him. Asked him if he would walk with us, hear us out. Mike told me that we could persuade Mathew not to talk to the police. We all agreed to walk up the hill together."

"The hill?"

"Constitution Hill."

"Right." Yvonne nodded. "Of course. Where Mathew died."

"Only, when we got up there, Mike got aggressive with Mathew. We all sat on a bench, looking out to sea. I thought Mike would work on persuading Mathew but, instead, he started yelling at him. Telling him that he had no ambition and couldn't see that we could get whatever we wanted."

"What happened then?"

"Mathew got up to go. He said there was no point in even trying to talk to Mike in that mood and he began walking away. Mike said we had to stop him. So, we grabbed hold of him. He struggled and I tried to talk to him. Mike grabbed Mathew's scarf and began pulling it tight around his neck. Mathew was gasping for air. I let go. I didn't want to be involved in any violence. I shouted for Mike to stop and I turned away, looking for help. I didn't see Mathew go off the cliff. But, I heard him cry out. When I turned back, Mike was walking towards me, carrying Matthew's scarf. He had a really black look on his face. I thought he was going to attack me."

"Did he? Did he hurt you?" Yvonne tilted her head in an attempt to see Benton's eyes beneath his lowered lids.

"No. He just said that Mathew had jumped off."

"But, you knew he hadn't jumped?"

"I didn't see what happened. I felt that Mike had pushed him off."

The door to the interview room burst open. DI Lucas was standing in the doorway. "Can I have a word?"

Yvonne pushed her chair back. Dewi accompanied her into the corridor.

"What are you doing talking to our witness?" DI Lucas glared at her. DS Lyons looked sheepish.

"He's our witness too and we've got him talking."

"You should have informed me."

"I thought the DCI telephoned you?"

"That's not the point. This is a sensitive investigation." He exhaled a large lungful of air. "Has he mentioned Vortex?"

Yvonne shook her head. "Not yet. I believe he was about to."

"Okay, well, we'll take it from here. You can go back to whatever you were doing."

That was it. They were dismissed.

Dewi looked as though he was about to argue but Yvonne nudged his elbow. "Come on. Let's go."

"But-"

"Let's go."

Dewi frowned, as they walked down the corridor away from the interview rooms. "What do we do now?"

"We go to Aberystwyth and talk to Mike. Take him to Aber station. You'll need your asp, cuffs and mace."

"Shouldn't we ask for backup?"

"Not yet." She paused, checking both ways along the corridor. "Listen, we're going to politely knock on the door and you're going to mimic Carantan's voice, asking to be let in."

Dewi pulled a face. "Why Carantan's?"

"It's a hunch. He opens the door and we arrest him. When we know where the children are, *then* we'll call for backup. If we have cars going up there now, Mike could be alerted and then god knows what might happen to the children. We've got to get this right."

"What about the DCI? You going to let him know?"

"When we get there, Dewi. When we get there."

Dewi let out a laugh. "You're madder than a box of frogs."

"And I'm desperate." Yvonne pursed her lips.

"Come on, then. Let's get our gear."

∼

THE FORTY-FIVE MINUTE journey to Aberystwyth seemed to take hours. Dewi drove. Yvonne had to remind herself to breathe. The saving grace was that there was little traffic on the road that time in the evening.

Yvonne rang the doorbell on the main door to the building and checked the door number for Mike. A girl's voice answered. "Yes?"

Dewi stepped forward. "It's Carl. I've come to see Mike."

The door buzzed open.

Yvonne gave Dewi a wink. "Well done."

As they climbed the stairs, Dewi had his hand inside his jacket, holding his baton. There was no-one on the landing.

Yvonne knocked gently on Mike's door.

Dewi cleared his throat. "It's Carl."

There was no answer.

Yvonne knocked again. No answer.

"He's gone out." A young male appeared in the doorway of the flat next door. Curly-haired and bare-footed. Strains of jazz music came from behind him.

"Oh. Do you know where?" Yvonne gave the lad a friendly smile.

"Er, I think he said he was going up the hill."

"Constitution Hill?"

"That's what he said."

"Okay. Well, thank you."

"Do you want me to pass on a message when he gets back?" The lad looked from Yvonne to Dewi and back again.

"Just tell him his aunt and uncle were looking for him."

29

THE CLIFFS

"He fell from here." Carantan peered down at the waves hitting the rocks below. "I wonder if he cried out." He turned to Mike. His voice only just raising above the sound of crashing water. "Did he? Did he cry out?"

"I don't know. I wasn't with him when he actually jumped."

"You told me you walked with him."

"I did. He told me he wanted to be by himself for a while."

Carantan's eyes were unblinking. "The police told me he suffered injuries that were not made when he hit those rocks."

Mike moved closer to Carantan. "What are you trying to say?"

"Did you kill Mathew?"

"Don't be stupid-"

"You did, didn't you? You hurt him and pushed him off the cliff. Didn't you?"

Mike's fist crashed into Carantan's jaw, knocking him over backwards.

Carantan picked himself up, shaking. He ran at Mike, who sidestepped and hit him again.

Carantan didn't fall this time but moved unsteadily in the direction of the pathway. He didn't see Mike approaching him with a large rock in his hand. It smashed into the back of his head and everything went dark.

Mike dragged the unconscious man's body towards the cliff.

∼

YVONNE AND DEWI walked calmly down the corridor, until the young lad had gone back inside his flat. At which point, they ran. Ten minutes later, they had parked at the bottom of the hill and were climbing the dimly-lit pathway.

Yvonne's insides quivered. Her mouth was dry. She took a deep breath.

"What's that?" Dewi asked in hushed tones, as he placed a hand on Yvonne's shoulder and pointed.

They had reached the top of the path and, silhouetted against the night sky, someone was dragging something towards the cliff.

"Let's go." Yvonne ran, quickly followed by her DS, who shone his torch at the silhouette.

"Stop! Police!" she yelled at the shape. "Mike? We need to talk to you."

Mike had hold of Carantan, who remained motionless. One push, and Carantan would be off the edge of the cliff.

Yvonne had a lump in her throat.

"Mike. Move away from Carl."

"He tried to kill me," Mike shouted. "Tried to push me off the cliff. I knocked him out. Thank goodness you-"

"Mike, we know about Mathew and we know about Vortex." She strained her voice, to lift it above the crashing waves below.

"Don't come any closer." Mike dropped Carantan and held up his mobile phone. "One call from me and the children will be toast."

"Was Vortex your idea, Mike? Or was it Benton's?" Yvonne kept her voice as even as she could.

"Benton? Ha." Mike tapped his forehead with his palm. "Benton couldn't have organised this. He's a tech guy. He has his uses, but planning? Never."

"How d'you come up with the idea? I mean, demanding ransom in Bitcoin, using the dark web. It was a smart move. Did you come up with all that?"

"Obviously." Mike moved towards them, still holding up his mobile phone. "You're going to let me go, now. I'm going to go down that path and you are going to let me go. If you make any attempt to chase me or, if I hear any police cars or helicopters, I press a button on this phone and the children will be gone. Are you hearing me? Gone."

Yvonne held up her hands. She could hear the waves smashing into the shoreline below.

She was still thinking about her next move when she felt searing pain shoot through the back of her head. Her world went dark.

30

CAPTIVE

When she came to, she was sat with her back to the wall and her hands cuffed, awkwardly, behind her. Tom and Sally were nuzzled into her stomach. As soon as they realised she was conscious, they became animated.

Tom put a tiny hand each side of her face. "Aunty Yvonne, Aunty Yvonne, Where's mummy? Is mummy coming?"

The room swam and her head hurt. She could feel blood down the side of her face. "Tom? Sally?"

"Aunty Yvonne. You woke up." Sally threw her arms around her aunt's abdomen. "Where *is* mummy?" she asked. "Is she coming, too? Did she come with you-"

"Are you okay?" A slurred male voice interjected.

She realised that Dewi was there with her. He was also cuffed.

"You were knocked unconscious." Dewi nodded towards the children, as though to say that he could not say much more in front of them. "The other children are here, too."

She looked across the room, where Peter held the torch,

·seated next to Donna, on a low bed. A young boy sat behind them, staring at her. She recognised him as Kyle.

"Peter, will you help me?" She could taste blood in the corner of her mouth.

"Sure. Er... What can I do?"

"She kicked off her left trainer.. There's a key. It's small-.It's taped to the inside of my trainer."

Dewi looked at her open-mouthed.

Peter hesitated.

"Go ahead. It's okay."

Peter pulled out the key.

"Now place it in the lock on these." She twisted around for him to access her cuffs. "You'll need to keep twisting til the second click."

As soon as Peter had freed her, she ran to dewi and released him from his cuffs.

"Do you always have a handcuffs key in your shoe?" He rubbed his wrists.

She shook her head."Not always. Just sometimes."

She kissed Tom and Sally and reassured them that they would be with their mummy soon. Then, taking each by the hand, she walked over to where the older children were seated. They appeared drained, their eyes hollow. Her heart went out to them. As she sat with them, she put her arms out to gather them all to her.

As Donna, Peter and a recovered Kyle filled in the gaps for her, Dewi paced over to the door, and began inspecting it. He came back to Peter, to borrow the torch. This left the rest of the room in darkness, aside from when the light illuminated it with intermittent flashes.With each flash, the DI learned a little more about their surroundings.

The room had a dusty, concrete floor. The walls were broken up by vertical concrete pillars. The door appeared to be solid iron and the bed had been fashioned from wooden pallets, pushed together. She decided they must be in an industrial warehouse. The lack of any noise from machinery suggested it was abandoned. She cuddled Tom and Sally tighter, her chin nuzzling each head in turn.

"Dead-locked." Dewi shook his head. "We'll have to wait until they come to us."

"They bring food and water once a day," Peter sighed. "They already brought it for today."

"What happened at the clifftop?" Yvonne asked Dewi.

"We were jumped from behind. I'm guessing by other members of Vortex. Mike must have been in touch with them after disabling Carantan."

The DI pursed her lips. "Did you get an idea of how many we are dealing with?"

"Five or six. Hard to say. They knocked you unconscious."

"Aunty, what's unconscious?" Tom asked.

Yvonne looked down at him, giving him a kiss on the top of his head. "It's when you're not really sure what's going on." She smiled at him and shook her head at Dewi, letting him know that it was okay and that it was best he did not say any more in front of the children. Dewi entertained the smaller children by pulling faces at them.

Yvonne stood up to stretch her legs and to think. Her thoughts were interrupted by the sound of voices and by keys rattling against the door.

She braced herself, fists clenched.

Dewi was up and by her side, as the door opened.

"Get back," they were ordered, and several men in dark clothing, holding metal pipes and flashlights, pushed into the room.

"Please, let us go." Yvonne took a pace forward, arms

outstretched, palms towards the men. "At least, let the children go. They have no idea who you are and are innocent in all this."

"Can't do that." Mike stepped forward, pulling off his black ski mask.

"What's the point of holding us?" Yvonne shook her head. "They have Benton. They have all his memory sticks and hard drives. It's only a matter of time before the tactical teams get here. Then, what will you do? Surely, it's better that you give up now than end up in a stand-off with officers who are armed to the teeth? You can't take this anywhere and you can't keep or convert the Bitcoin you have made. You-"

"Shut up! Just... Shut up." Mike ran his hand through his hair, his eyes flicking from side-to-side as he considered his next move. "We're getting out of here."

"All of us?"

"Yes."

Tom and Sally cried, holding her aunt's legs.

"Please, let them go," Yvonne pleaded again.

"Just take *me*." Dewi held his wrists out. "Let them go."

"Not a chance. You're *all* our insurance. You're *all* getting in the van."

∼

THERE WERE no seats in the back of the transit van. They sat on the bare, ridged-metal floor. Every bone in their body jolted, as the abductors drove at speed. Yvonne did her best to protect Tom and Sally from the worst of it, seating them on her legs whilst she held them in her arms. They cried for the first ten minutes, then fell silent, clinging to her as though their lives depended on it.

At the back, next to the van doors, two of the abductors sat in silence. Yvonne took a good look at their eyes. The rest of their faces were hidden inside ski masks. One of them had dark eyes and long lashes. The other's eyes were hazel and his lashes were shorter. He had a small scar through his right eyebrow. She committed it to memory.

"Where are you taking us?" Although he knew the question would be futile, Dewi asked it anyway. Yvonne wondered if it helped take his mind off the pain which must be developing in his back from bouncing around in the van.

As expected, there no reply. Yvonne looked over, and he gave her a smile that was meant to reassure her. She feared for the children. Their abductors were now desperate men.

As she kissed the top of Sally's head, she heard sirens. Faint, but definitely sirens. She held her breath, her body stiffening. The sirens became louder, and overhead, the unmistakable sound of a helicopter.

The van veered wildly, throwing its occupants this way and that. The children started to cry again. Yvonne braced herself against the van wall so that she could hold them steady. She prayed they did not to crash.

Dewi was holding his lower back and she knew he must be in considerable pain. Still, he did his best not to show it. Had there been only one guard in the back, she knew he would have tried his luck. With two, the odds were too high. Especially, given they had such young children present. Instead, Dewi placed a calming hand on Peter's shoulder. The young boy pressed his lips into a thin line, casting murderous looks towards their guards.

Donna sat comforting Kyle who, although his health had considerably improved, said little. His eyes followed everything from under his overlong fringe.

A sound like a muffled explosion and they were all

thrown forward. Yvonne realised police stingers must have been used. The chain of spikes had perforated the van's tyres, sending it skidding to a grinding halt.

Dewi steadied himself and lurched at the two men at the back who had also been thrown off balance. Peter joined in.

Yvonne moved the two youngest children to the opposite end of the van and stood between them and the fight, looking for any opportunity to help Dewi and Peter.

The van doors were almost ripped off their hinges, and several armed officers piled in to grab the abductors, who were still grappling with Dewi and Peter.

Yvonne's knees failed her and she collapsed to the floor.

31

AFTERMATH

They were taken to Bronglais hospital in Aberystwyth and checked over. All were discharged soon afterwards, with the exception of Kyle Jenkins, who was to be kept in overnight for observation. His parents joined him and had to be reminded on numerous occasions that their excited chatter might not be what Kyle needed. Yvonne noticed how his eyes shone, however, and knew that he was going to be okay.

Tom and Sally travelled back with Yvonne, in a specially laid-on police vehicle, to their mum. Kim was beside herself with happiness and kissed them repeatedly, whilst they tried to tell her about their adventures. They would be telling those stories into a video camera later in the week. Evidence that would help see Vortex members jailed for a considerable length of time. Yvonne closed her eyes, thankful that her nephew and niece were back where they belonged. As soon as their mum paused for breath, their aunt threw her arms around them and held them tight against her heart.

She had feared the worst in regard to Carl Carantan,

motionless at the top of the cliff. Dewi informed her, however, that he was alive and had simply been unconscious. After coming round, he had staggered, bruised and bleeding, down Constitution Hill, where he had been helped by passers by. He was admitted to hospital, but his injuries were not serious.

THE NEXT DAY, Yvonne contacted Shelter and social services on behalf of Donna and the other residents of Benton's Llanidloes house. Since he would be spending some time in prison, they would need all the help they could get in being either rehoused or reunited

with long-lost family.

Lucas and Lyons congratulated her in locating the hostages. They claimed they had also been at the point of tracking them down, having found out that Benton was being blackmailed by Mike Jones. It was Benton who had given them Donna's location, prior to her abduction.

The DI had one more thing left to do. She telephoned Carantan at his department in the university.

"Carantan."

"Doctor Carantan, it's Yvonne Giles."

"Oh." He paused, as though searching for the right words. "I hear you saved my life." He cleared his throat. "I read it in this morning's newspaper."

"You were unconscious, the last time I saw you."

"And I would have been off the edge of that cliff."

From the slow way he said the words, she could picture his eyes, soulful. "Mathew didn't kill himself. It was Mike, wasn't it?"

"Yes, it was. I didn't figure it out until you and your sergeant came to see me that day. What you said, about the injuries, it all made sense. I challenged Mike about it and what you witnessed was the aftermath."

"I'm so sorry." Yvonne sighed into the phone.

"You suspected me, didn't you?" His voice held no malice.

"For a while," Yvonne admitted. "I wish you well, Doctor Carantan. But please, keep a better eye on your students."

He gave a muted laugh. "Don't worry, Inspector. I'll be monitoring their every move from now on. And... Yvonne? Thank you."

THE END

AFTERWORD

If you enjoyed this book, I would be very grateful if you would post a short review on Amazon or Goodreads. Your support really does make a difference.

Mailing list: You can join my emailing list here : AnnamarieMorgan.com

Facebook page: AnnamarieMorganAuthor

You might also like to read the other books in the series:

Book 1: Death Master

After months of mental and physical therapy, Yvonne Giles, an Oxford DI, is back at work and that's just how she likes it. So when she's asked to hunt the serial killer responsible for taking apart young women, the DI jumps at the chance but hides the fact she is suffering debilitating flashbacks. She is told to work with Tasha Phillips, an in-her-face, criminal psychologist. The DI is not enamoured with the idea. Tasha has a lot to prove. Yvonne has a lot to get over. A tentative link with a 20 year-old cold case brings them closer to the truth but events then take a horrifyingly personal turn.

Book 2: You Will Die

After apprehending an Oxford Serial Killer, and almost losing her life in the process, DI Yvonne Giles has left England for a quieter life in rural Wales.Her peace is shattered when she is asked to hunt a priest-killing psychopath, who taunts the police with messages inscribed on the corpses.Yvonne requests the help of Dr. Tasha Phillips, a psychologist and friend, to aid in the hunt. But the killer is one step ahead and the ultimatum, he sets them, could leave everyone devastated.

Book 3: Total Wipeout

A whole family is wiped out with a shotgun. At first glance, it's an open-and-shut case. The dad did it, then killed himself. The deaths follow at least two similar family wipeouts – attributed to the financial crash.

So why doesn't that sit right with Detective Inspector Yvonne Giles? And why has a rape occurred in the area, in the weeks preceding each family's demise? Her seniors do not believe there are questions to answer. DI Giles must therefore risk everything, in a high-stakes investigation of a mysterious masonic ring and players in high finance.

Can she find the answers, before the next innocent family is wiped out?

Book 4: Deep Cut

In a tiny hamlet in North Wales, a female recruit is murdered whilst on Christmas home leave. Detective Inspector Yvonne Giles is asked to cut short her own leave, to investigate. Why was the young soldier killed? And is her death related to several alleged suicides at her army base? DI Giles this it is, and that someone powerful has a dark secret they will do anything to hide.

Book 5: The Pusher

Young men are turning up dead on the banks of the River Severn. Some of them have been missing for days or even weeks. The only thing the police can be sure of, is that the men have drowned.

Rumours abound that a mythical serial killer has turned his attention from the Manchester canal to the waterways of Mid-Wales.

And now one of CID's own is missing. A brand new police recruit with everything to live for. DI Giles must find him before it's too late.

Coming Soon:
Book 6: The Crossbow Killer

Printed in Great Britain
by Amazon